BLOOD JUNGLE

ERIC S. BROWN

SEVEREDPRESS

BLOOD JUNGLE

ISBN: 978-1-922861-39-9

BLOOD JUNGLE

The blast of a .44 Magnum thundered. The tied together finger bones of the necklace worn by the tribesman clacked and rattled against one another as his corpse dropped into the thick foliage covering the jungle floor, a gaping hole blown through the center of his chest.

James cursed, tossing the revolver away. The bullet he put in the tribesman had been his last. His plan had been to save the round for his own skull. Killing himself was a hell of a lot better option than what the group chasing had in mind for his future. Instinct had gotten the better of him when the tribesman leaped out at him. There had been no time to think, no time to react any other way.

The rich bastards James led out here in search of adventure their cash couldn't buy them in the city were already dead. James told himself that he had done all that was possible to save them but knew that was a lie. He'd left them to die. That was a plain and cold, hard fact. It didn't matter now though. All that mattered was staying alive.

Voices rang out from behind him, constantly drawing closer, no matter how fast he ran. The tribesmen knew this jungle better. It was their home. He was the outsider and the one who was lost. James had lost his bearing during the ambush. Given a chance, he could likely find them again but for now his flight was blind. All James knew was that he heading South towards the river.

The tribesmen chasing him were cannibals. James had known there'd been a chance of encountering them coming here but the pay'd been too good to turn down. This single trip into the jungle was supposed to have been enough to buy him months off without the need to take another gig but there was no one left to pay him now.

Suddenly, the trees parted ahead of him. James burst out of the jungle onto the riverbank. He skidded to a halt, sucking in a startled breath, blinking his eyes. The sun stung his eyes, so much brighter gleaming off the moving water of the river. James didn't see the cannibal coming at him until it was too late. The man slammed into him, screaming, knife raised. James' right hand shot up and out, catching the man's knife hand by the wrist to keep the blade from plunging down into him as the two of them toppled from the bank into the river with a loud splash.

They wrestled there, thrashing about, evenly matched in strength. Rolling about in the mud at the river's edge, their bodies twisted in strained effort to overpower the other, neither of them saw that they weren't alone.

Ridged, yellow eyes rested slightly above the waterline, watching them. . . then those eyes rose upwards as the creature they belonged to stood up on two legs. The cannibal shrieked in pain as the claws of the thing's far too human-like hands sunk into his back, lifting him away from James and out of the water. With a quick jerk, the creature ripped the cannibal apart, separating his top half from his bottom, in an explosion of blood and gore. Red splattered down over James as he stared at the monster towering above him in utter shock. He'd heard the legends, the stories whispered in the backrooms of the seedier bars he liked to frequent but had never believed them.

James turned his back to the monster, desperately

trying to scale the muddy river bank as fast as he could. Above him were several of the cannibals. Despite their fierce face paint, the expressions they wore were ones of fear. Behind James, the thing in the water let out a deep, rattling roar. The cannibals fled, disappearing into the jungle as his hands grasped at the mud of the bank trying to heave himself up it to the shore.

The creature grabbed James by the back of his shirt and hurled him out into the water of the river. James splashed into it, plunging beneath the surface of the water. His head came bursting back up, gasping for air, as the creature waded calmly in his direction, sinking into the river with him. As it vanished beneath the surface, James was already making a beeline for the shore down river from where the creature had been.

He'd never seen anything like it in his life. There were stories of such a creature that were told in the local bars and back alleys but James always thought they were just another crappy bunch of tales made up to scare off those that weren't welcome in the region. Never in a billion years would he have thought something like that thing in the water with him now could actually exist.

The creature darted between James and the shore

with impossible speed then came straight at him. James twisted in the water, trying to dodge the thing, but it slammed into him, thickly muscled arms wrapping about his waist. He struggled against its hold on him, bashing his fists with all the force he could muster into its back. Hitting the creature was like hitting a brick wall. His blows seemed to have no effect whatsoever on it but they tore the hell out of his hands. The scales that covered the thing's body cut and slashed at his skin with each blow James struck.

James had sucked in a breath before the creature plowed into him but even so his lungs were burning now as the creature rolled him over and over in the current of the river, taking him deeper and deeper, down towards the bottom. James' vision blurred as the thing's grip on him tightened then in a burst of bubbles, what air was left in his lungs exploded out. His body shook and jerked, still being dragged further downward by the creature, as dirty river water rushed in to replace the air he had expelled. The last thing James saw before he lost consciousness was the creature's yellow eyes glowing in the darkness of the murky water.

****

Jagger's hands were clammy. It was the only outward sign of the intensity of his emotional state as he watched Migel and Yondo holding Roberto's arms tight behind his back. Marcola stood in front of them, his eyes burning with rage. The ACJ 220 they were all aboard belonged to him. Marcola was the head of one of the largest cartels in South America and the expense and luxury of the plane reflected that. Jagger figured the jet had to be one of the largest and certainly the most advanced being used currently to smuggle drugs into the United States.

The ACJ 220 had six zones - the pilot compartment, a spacious and luxurious relaxation area with a full bar, Marcola's personal quarters, and two large storage sections. Jagger couldn't even imagine what a jet like the ACJ 220 cost even without all the modifications Marcola had built into it. The jet's systems were totally pimped out with stealth tech, hidden armor plating. . . hell, the thing even had a secret air to air missile launcher built into its belly in case of a dire emergency where escape was not an option. It was a symbol of Marcola's importance in the cartel world and of his power.

Roberto grunted as Marcola punched him in the

stomach, doubling over as much as he could, given that Migel and Yondo were holding him in place. His face was already a mess, beaten bloody, with several teeth missing, lips swollen and cut. Marcola hadn't soiled his own hands with that work though. He'd left it to Juan, the hulking giant that served as his personal bodyguard and right-hand man. Now that hard work was done though, Marcola was adding a personal touch to Roberto's torture. The cartel leader was both angered and insulted by discovering that a federal agent had slipped into his ranks. Roberto spat blood onto the floor, raising his head slowly, with great effort, to look at Marcola. For a moment, Jagger was worried Roberto was about to say something and make matters even worse for himself. He didn't though.

In all, there were eighteen people aboard the jet, counting the two pilots. What Marcola didn't know was that Roberto wasn't the only undercover agent among them. Yuri, one of the pilots, and Jagger, himself, too were also working for the United States government. The three of them had all infiltrated Marcola's organization at different times in different ways but they were all here now. They'd discovered each other and began working together long before Marcola even suspected his crew had been infiltrated. The plan was simple; they intended to bust Marcola the second the ACJ 220 set down on US soil. Of course that was before Marcola figured out who and what Roberto was.

Roberto was as good as dead. There wasn't a fragging thing Jagger could do to help Roberto. Even with six of Marcola's men in the rear zones of the jet where the drugs were being stored, and another up front in the pilot compartment with Yuri, that left him facing not just Marcola but seven armed cartel men and women, who dealing out death and pain came second nature to. His training told him that he shouldn't even be thinking about trying but still it was hard for Jagger to just stand there, watching the hell Roberto was going through. Part of him wished Marcola would just hurry up and finish him.

"You come into my house!" Marcola raged, "You lie to my face! Threaten my business and my family!"

Marcola shook his head. "A quick death is far too good for a swine like you, federale!"

Snapping his fingers, Marcola gestured to Juan.

The giant came lumbering over and handed his boss a gardening pruner. Marcola usually used them for trimming the small trees he kept in his personal quarters aboard the jet. The cartel leader accepted them with a feral grin parting his lips.

Marcola motioned for Javier, another of his men, to come to him. There was fear in Javier's eyes but he did as Marcola indicated. Jagger saw Javier relax as Marcola passed the pruners onto him. Everyone knew that Marcola suspected Roberto wasn't working alone and Javier had to have been worried that the cartel leader thought him to be an agent too.

Javier walked to Roberto as Migel and Yondo forced one of his hands out so that it could be gotten at. Grabbing hold of Roberto's extended hand, Javier went for the trigger finger. There was a splash of red and the crunch of breaking bone as Javier relieved Roberto of it. Roberto howled in pain, blood spurting from where his finger had been.

Marcola was laughing. The sound of that was more sickening to Jagger than the snapping of bone as Roberto's finger came off. He kept his expression cold and professional.

"Another," Marcola ordered Javier. "Go on. Have some fun."

Roberto's bird finger thudded to the floor next to where his trigger finger lay. Javier worked his way across Roberto's entire right hand leaving only the thumb still attached to it. Blood was pouring from the stubs of what remained of his fingers.

"Good! Good!" Marcola cackled and motioned for Javier to step away from the federal agent.

"I bet that hurts, you bastard," Marcola snarled, grabbing him by his hair and jerking Roberto's head so that he was looking up at him. "Still too good for such as you but what is one to do? The human body can only endure so much. Wouldn't want you passing out on us yet. No, not when you've yet to tell us who your friends are among my ranks."

Roberto said nothing and the expression he wore didn't either.

"Oh yes, federale, I know there are more of your filth in my home," Marcola sneered. "Even aboard this jet. And I will find out who they are whether you tell me or not."

Roberto, on his knees and hurting, managed a feral grin of his own. "Sometimes Marcola, taking down men like you is worth more noble blood being spilled."

Jagger's heart skipped a beat inside his chest as Roberto very clearly looked in his direction. The bastard had just screwed him over. There was no way in hell that Marcola had missed it. The implication of Roberto's glance at him had sealed his fate. Jagger knew he would be next once the cartel leader finished with Roberto. Why? Why would Roberto damn him like that? Then, it hit him. The words Roberto said echoed inside his head.

"Oh frag," Jagger muttered, knowing what Roberto must have done.

"Why are you smiling?" Marcola spat in Roberto's face. "Why?"

"Boom," Roberto whispered just loud enough for Marcola to hear.

And then everything went to hell. The jet shook as something in its rear zones blew. A second explosion followed from somewhere forward of the zone they were in and then another. Jagger was flung from his feet. He landed, hard, on the floor, making a grab for the closest seat. His fingers caught it, latching on. Most of the others weren't so lucky. They were tossed around, smacked against the walls and in some cases each other. Roberto broke free of Migel and Yondo's hold on him, trying to flee into the next zone of the jet beyond the one they were all in. Marcola didn't let that happen. The cartel leader drew a gold plated .45 from beneath his jacket and fired a shot that pierced Roberto's forehead, right above his eyes, sending brain matter and bone fragments splattering into the air. Roberto's body crumpled, thudding onto the floor to roll about there with the shifting and bouncing of the jet.

"Everyone grab something and hold on!" Yuri's voice rang out of the jet's intercom. "We're going down!"

The zone around Jagger shifted as the jet angled downward. He held tight to the seat his hands clutched. Everyone was screaming and shouting. Even Marcola was now. The cartel leader was demanding that Juan get to the pilot compartment and find out what was going on or rather what had happened. The damage was done. Roberto had seen to that, Jagger figured. He'd clearly planted the I.E.D.s that had detonated. His role as one of the members of Marcola's crew that oversaw the security of the ACJ 220 give him the access to do it. Now they were all going to pay for Marcola's crimes, himself and Yuri included.

****

Yuri woke up screaming, his eyes wide. It took him a second to realize that the jet was down now. He turned his head to look at Harrison, his co-pilot.

Harrison was shoved upright in his seat, pinned back by the limb of a tree that reached through the shattered, forward window to impale him. Yuri could see a good three feet of the limb protruding from the back of Harrison's seat.

It hadn't been a nightmare. They'd really gone down. Yuri sucked in a breath. Doing so hurt like Hell but he didn't give a frag, Yuri was just happy to be alive. He remembered it all now. The explosions that came out of nowhere, punching holes in the jet's body, and blowing its left wing engine to bits of carbon scored metal, leaving the right barely functional. He and Harrison had fought with everything they had to keep that remaining engine going long enough to bring them in for the best controlled landing they could manage. There were no clearings, much less landing fields, in the jungle they had been over. The jet had come down hard. Wasn't anything they could do to change that. But he and Harrison did manage to keep the jet mostly intact and minimize the damage to the extent that they could. Their efforts hadn't saved Harrison. Yuri's emotions were mixed on that. Sure, the guy worked for perhaps the largest drug cartel in South America but Harrison was only a pilot, not a hired gun or dealer out on the streets.

Releasing the safety harness that held him in his seat, Yuri examined his own body. His ribs ached as his hands patted over and probed them. They were bruised but nothing more. He was a bit banged up but that was all. Yuri thought about just how much of a miracle that was, looking over at Harrison again.

Heaving himself to his feet, Yuri decided that acting more hurt than he felt was likely a smart thing to do. The door that led into the jet's first zone was closed but there was still some power in the jet's systems. He stabbed the button on the wall that opened the door. It slid sideways. Yuri stumbled through. It was utterly trashed. Broken glass belonging to the bottles that had been displayed behind the bar was everywhere. Part of the interior ceiling had collapsed inward, electrical cables and loose wiring dangled downward out of it. Sparks flew here and there among them. There were no open flames . . . yet.

Migel rushed up to him, shoving Yuri. He staggered, colliding painfully with the wall.

"What the hell you do, man?" Migel raged, raising a fist to strike him. Yuri, wide eyed, was scared to defend himself, as he knew what had been going on back here with Roberto. He didn't want to do anything that could reveal himself if Roberto hadn't told them who he was. Yuri had already spotted Roberto's body as he entered. The guy was dead, brains blown out of his skull.

Juan came bounding across the zone, one of his huge hands grabbing Migel by the throat. The giant slammed Migel into the wall with such force that it bent from the man's impact.

"You leave him alone, Migel!" Juan roared. "This man just saved us all!"

Migel, clearly hurting, squirmed against the giant's grip. "What you mean? He . . ."

"He saved us, you idiot!" Juan bellowed. "If not for his flying, none of us would be alive! You think anyone could bring in a jet with its engines in flames as intact as Yuri just did? Now, you leave him be or we'll be having a much more serious discussion about the matter, Migel. You understand me?"

Migel nodded and Juan's fingers released his throat allowing him to slide to the floor.

"Thank you," Yuri told Juan, utterly stunned to receive help from such an unlikely source.

"You saved us, pilot man," Juan grunted. "I know this."

Yuri swallowed and kept his mouth shut,

thumping a friendly soft tap on Juan's arm while flashing the giant a sincerely thankful smile.

Looking around, Yuri saw that Roberto wasn't the only one who was dead. Yondo was dead too. His crumpled body lay against the far wall, neck bent at an unnatural angle, blood slowly dripping from his open mouth.

"Yuri!" Marcola shouted at him, coming his way. "Good to see you made it, muchacho!"

"Thank you, sir," Yuri answered, hiding his nerves. He hadn't been in a position that required him to interact with Marcola much. Certainly not on the level that Jagger or even Roberto did.

"I am going to have to give you a raise!" Marcola cackled, "After I buy you a new plane of course."

Yuri remained silent, keeping a dumb grin on his face as Marcola went on.

"Do you know, did we come apart on the way down?" Marcola asked. "Is the whole jet still intact?"

Marcola's words triggered what little memories Yuri had of the last readouts from the 220's systems before impact. The controls had been too damaged from the crash to tell him anything after he'd woken up or at least that's what he told himself. He'd been too shaken up to even think of checking them.

"Mostly intact, sir," Yuri answered. "There are some breaches in her hull but she didn't break up. Harrison and I brought her in as easy as we could."

"And Harrison?" Marcola eyed him.

"Dead, sir," Yuri told the cartel leader. "He was killed in the crash."

Marcola clicked his lips.

"Too bad," Marcola said and then grinned, slapping him on the arm, "Good thing we still have you then, eh, Yuri? Tell me, how is the comm.? Were you able to get out a call for help?"

Yuri hadn't. A jet hauling such a large cargo of drugs to the States couldn't just put out a general call for help regardless. Marcola's people were the only folks he could have radioed but frankly, there hadn't been time. It had taken everything just to bring the 220 in like he had.

"Not that was answered," Yuri winced, putting a hand against his bruised ribs.

"I see," Marcola snorted. "Is the equipment still operable?"

Yuri shook his head. "There is some power left in the jet's systems, sir, but the comms are out. What power we do have isn't going to last long though."

"Can you repair the damage, make the comms work?" Marcola asked.

"It's too extensive," Yuri said. "And I don't have the parts that would be needed to do it either. There's not even anything here to jury rig something with."

Yuri sweated bullets as Marcola looked him over, anger boiling in his eyes. Finally, Marcola sighed, apparently deciding that hurting him would gain them nothing.

"So, we are on our own then?" Marcola pressed.

Yuri nodded.

Marcola took it much better than he'd expected. The cartel leader shrugged and simply said, "Such is life, I guess. The cargo will be safe here at least until we can get out of this jungle and return for it."

Not having any idea how Marcola reached that conclusion, Yuri merely nodded again, agreeing with him.

"You have first aid training, no?" Marcola suddenly growled at him, mood switching so quickly it was like he was bipolar. "Get to work helping those that you can get in shape for the march out of this damned place!"

"Yes sir!" Yuri yelped.

"Juan, you help him," Marcola barked at his

giant bodyguard.

Yuri felt one of Juan's massive hands on his back, shoving him in the direction of where the emergency first aid kit was located on the rear wall of the zone. He caught one last glimpse of Marcola as the cartel leader vanished into the next zone that served as his personal quarters. Maria and Shonda went with Marcola.

"He didn't ask me where we were?" Yuri stammered.

"Does it matter?" Juan asked. "We're somewhere in the jungle, likely near the Amazon River, I would reckon. Regardless, there will be no help coming so all we can do is march out ourselves but of course first, we'll have to track down that bastard that got away after the crash."

"What?" Yuri's eyes bugged.

"Roberto wasn't working alone," Juan shrugged. "If you find one rat, there are always more. Turns out that Jagger was apparently a Fed too. Roberto gave him away before setting off whatever crap he'd rigged up to blow the hell out of this jet. Guess the bastard figured we would all die when it went down."

Then Juan suddenly gave a cheerful laugh. "Good thing Roberto underestimated just what a pilot you are!"

"No way!" Yuri exclaimed, faking as much shock as he could as he seemed to fully process what the big man had just told him. "Jagger's a Fed?"

The giant nodded, frowning, "Si. And he got away too somehow during the crash or right after, just slipped out that hole over there."

Yuri saw the hole in the zone for the first time. It wasn't large but was certainly there. Something had scraped at the jet as it had bounced and skidded to a stop leaving a hole just large enough for a desperate man to squeeze through. Yuri could see bright sunlight spilling into the jet through it. Blinking, Yuri wiped at the sweat on his brow. Good for Jagger, he thought, at least he's got a chance out there. If it hadn't been for the dumb luck of this zone being damaged in such a manner, Marcola would likely have shot him already. Carrying on his own deception should be easy enough as long as he didn't do anything stupid.

With Juan at his side to help when needed, Yuri worked among the survivors of the crash, tending their wounds as best he could with his limited training and supplies. Some resisted out of pride or shock but Juan made sure they submitted, that resistance was useless. Everyone got what help Yuri could give them. Thankfully, most were just banged up. Yondo was the worst off of the lot. His left arm had been broken too badly for Yuri to even attempt to set. Yondo self-medicated with some cocaine from his personal stash and Juan let him be. Yuri didn't say anything to Yondo about it. The cocaine was a hell of a lot better than nothing for the pain he had to be in.

When their rounds were finished, Juan laid a massive hand on Yuri's shoulder.

"You did good work, amigo," the giant assured Yuri.

Yuri was sweating and exhausted, his own bruises hurting like hell.

"Thanks," Yuri managed a weak smile. "Gotta do what the boss tells you to, ya know?"

"Always," Juan's hand squeezed him where it rested on his shoulder. "But you can't rest yet, Yuri."

Yuri frowned. "Why?"

"You need to come with me," Juan said and led Yuri into Marcola's private zone of the jet.

Marcola was resting on his bed, Maria lying with him. Shonda sat in a chair on its far side, picking at her nails with a wicked looking knife. Izan was there too. Juan might be Marcola's bodyguard and right-hand man but it was Izan that served as the cartel leader's advisor and, when needed, hitman.

Izan gave Yuri the creeps. The guy was colder than anything living had a right to be. He wasn't a musclebound giant like Juan but there was death in his eyes. Izan was lean but far from weak. Yuri had heard stories about just how lethal the assassin was. Despite Juan's size and strength, Yuri would put his money on Izan as the winner if the two ever fought. Izan's arms were covered from the wrist of each hand to his shoulder with tattoos of spiraling dragons. His eyes were a bright, fiercely intelligent green and his face hard as stone.

Yuri wondered why he was being included in a meeting on the level of what was surely about to take place. He had to be careful. One slip up and Yuri knew he would share Roberto's fate.

"Ah. . .Juan, Yuri," Marcola beamed at the pilot and giant as they entered. "I am glad you're here. I was beginning to think I'd have to dispatch Izan to bring you in."

"Sorry boss," Juan grunted. "There was a lot to do out there."

Marcola waved a hand dismissively. "No more about that now. We've much more important things to discuss."

"Like how the hell we're gonna get out of here," Shonda added.

Marcola shot her a look but let her be otherwise.

"Yes," Marcola nodded. "That. And more. We must find and eliminate Jagger. That is a necessary first step."

Yuri noticed Izan give a sharp nod.

"As you are all aware, it's more than a matter of personal honor," Marcola smirked. "Jagger must be dealt with. We cannot afford to trust the jungle alone to ensure this for us."

The room was quiet. No one disputed the cartel leader.

"Seeing him dead is our first priority followed closely by figuring out how to get back to civilization alive. I'm no fool. I know how dangerous these jungles can be. Even the damn bugs can kill you if luck doesn't go your way," Marcola told them all. "Yuri, just how far will we need to travel?"

Now it made sense why Juan had brought him into the meeting. Marcola assumed that he must know exactly where they had come down. Yuri didn't but he had a close enough guess.

"We'll need to head north," Yuri answered.

"That will be the shortest route. I'd wager if we push ourselves and make good time combined with leaving the cargo here to return for later, it'll take six, maybe seven days on foot."

Marcola frowned but didn't get angry at the news. "That is a long time to be out here. Do we have enough supplies to make that kind of walk?"

"Supplies can be rationed," Shonda snorted, "And if we follow closely to the river, water won't be a problem. We have purifying tablets on board and there's always the option of simply straining and boiling the river water as well."

"If we should lose some men along the way, that would not be the worst thing that's ever happened," Izan commented.

"I'd prefer not to," Marcola looked at the killer. "But as needs must. We shall see how things go with the supplies and the journey. Yuri, do you know anything about this place where we've found ourselves?"

"If my judgement of where we've come down is correct then this area is supposed to be home to one of the last cannibal tribes," Yuri answered.

Even Izan cocked an eyebrow at that news. Shonda sat up straighter in her chair. Maria let out a whimper while Marcola muttered a curse too quiet for Yuri to make out clearly.

"Cannibals?" Juan's deep voice boomed, repeating the word.

Yuri nodded. "No one really knows more than that. I can't tell you how many of them we could run into or the exact borders of their turf here."

Marcola suddenly laughed. Yuri didn't know if it was a front or if the cartel leader's concern had truly vanished as he thought things over.

"A primitive tribe is no threat to us," Marcola boasted. "We are heavily armed and thanks to you, Yuri, aware of their presence now. If they come at us, they will not find us wanting. We'll show them that no one. . . no one messes with the cartel!"

"Right," Juan agreed. "I shall make sure the men know to keep an eye as we travel."

"Yes. Do so," Marcola ordered. "I want us all to be ready to leave by tomorrow morning. In the meantime, Juan, you and Izan are charged with locating Mr. Jagger and relieving him of his life. Take however many men you need so long as at least a few remain to keep us safe here."

"Will do," Juan motioned for Izan to come with him and they left Marcola's quarters together.

"What about me, boss?" Yuri asked.

"Go. Find out everything else you can about

where we have landed before the power goes completely out," Marcola said.

"Consider me on it," Yuri nodded and followed the giant and hitman out.

****

Jagger limped through the jungle. He was royally, fragging screwed and knew it. When Roberto detonated whatever the hell he'd rigged to blow the ACJ 220 out of the sky, he'd likely killed them all. Part of Jagger hated him for it though he understood what Roberto must have been thinking. Roberto must have caught wind that he was about to be discovered before it happened and the explosives were his last, desperate means of striking back at Marcola and the cartel. If the drug lord couldn't be brought to justice in the States then blowing him to bits must have seemed an acceptable alternative. Of course, doing so would mean taking both him and Yuri along to hell too as part of the process. Frag Roberto for making that call without at least trying to let them know what his plan had been.

When the jet crashed, tearing through the jungle, its hull had been breached in several places. Thank God one had been in the main zone of the plane. Jagger found himself in a good place to make use of it. As soon as everything had stopped moving, he was through it and running for his life. He'd heard the crack of a pistol and bullet thud into the wall above the hole behind him. Whoever fired at him, most likely Marcola himself, had been too slow.

Getting out of the jet might have been a break of good luck but nothing else about his situation was. His leg wasn't broken but was banged up fairly badly from the drop out of the jet to the jungle floor though it was mainly caused by how he landed, not the height. It hurt with every step Jagger took and wasn't getting any better. He needed to rest and take a better look at it. Jagger also knew he needed to find some kind of shelter before nightfall or at least a means of getting up off the jungle floor. He knew enough about the Amazon rainforest to know that nearly everything in it was deadly. Sleeping on the ground with the ants, other insects, and snakes wasn't something that should be done if it could be helped. Right now though, Jagger was still focused on putting as much distance between himself and the crashed jet as possible. There wasn't a chance in hell that Marcola would just let him go and hope the jungle got him. The cartel leader couldn't risk it. If he got out of the jungle alive with everything he knew about Marcola and his operation to testify in a court of law, it would be the end of everything for the drug lord.

On the upside, he still had his twin, engraved Colt .45s and an extra magazine for each of them. That gave him forty rounds and a much better chance of survival than Jagger had any right to after such a remote plane crash. If he ran into some kind of predator or trouble with a local clan of tribesmen, at least he would be able to defend himself.

Jagger paused for a moment, using the backside of his right hand to wipe at the sweat on his brow. The day was hot as hell and the humidity of the jungle only made it worse. He'd lost all track of time. Checking his watch, Jagger saw that it was close to 4 PM. The sun would be setting a lot sooner than he'd thought. Cursing, Jagger lurched forward again, hobbling onward, his injured leg sending bursts of pain throughout him with every step he took.

Looking up at the sky, Jagger figured he was heading south. That was good. Most likely, Marcola and the others would head north. That direction would likely be the shortest route towards somewhere with civilization and a means for them to get help. Of course, Marcola and the others wouldn't set out that way until they came after him.

Jagger knew that the cartel leader would dispatch Izan and a group to make sure he was dead first. Izan was a professional killer but Jagger knew the man wasn't any more trained to operate in a jungle like this than he was. That gave Jagger some hope. With a bit of luck, maybe he could avoid Izan and whoever else Marcola sent with him entirely.

Jagger wondered if Yuri had survived the crash. He hadn't seen the pilot since before the ACJ 220 had taken off. Had Yuri known about what Roberto rigged up in case he was found out? Hell, was Yuri even still alive? The front of the plane looked to have taken the most damage from what he'd seen, looking back at it, as he ran for his life. If Yuri did survive the crash, what was he doing now? Had the pilot been found out like Roberto and himself or was Yuri's cover still intact? Regardless, there wasn't anything Yuri could do to help him even if the pilot was still alive short of perhaps misleading Marcola and the others about the area the jet had come down in. Jagger hoped Yuri was okay. The man was a good agent.

Stopping again, Jagger spotted a downed tree lying on the jungle floor and headed for it. It was a place he could catch a breath. Jagger sat on the tree, getting his weight off his injured leg for the first time during his trek through the jungle. A sigh of relief escaped him. He noticed there was blood on his pants. It wasn't bad. Jagger inspected his injury. His leg was badly bruised from the top of his hip to his knee. There were several scratches, none so deep as to be worrisome other than the risk of infection. And his leg would get infected if he couldn't find a means to clean up his wounds. He needed to find some water but even if he did, Jagger wondered if he could risk building the fire that would be needed to boil it.

He sat on the downed tree for a while, occasionally glancing up at the sky, as the rays of the sun grew dimmer. The sun would likely be setting in less than a couple of hours. Heaving himself to his feet, Jagger got moving again, continuing southward. As he did so, Jagger heard movement in the jungle behind him. He whirled about, drawing his pistols with the speed and skill of an O West gunfighter. They cleared their holsters, almost in a blur, ready for action. He had been expecting to see Izan and a group of cartel thugs but they weren't there. Jagger's eyes darted about, searching for a target. Jagger didn't see anything, nothing that could have made the noise he'd heard.

Not even daring to breathe, Jagger stood his ground, continuing to look around. The jungle was quiet except for the buzzing of distant insects. And still, nothing moved in the direction the noise he'd heard came from. Jagger grunted as a slight breeze passed over him. On it was a stench so horrid and disgusting, Jagger nearly doubled over. Jagger's stomach heaved and bile rose up into his throat. He fought down the sickness through sheer force of will.

Without warning, something came flying out of the depths of the jungle at him. Jagger's pistols cracked in rapid succession. He put three rounds into the thing coming at him before flinging himself out of its path. The brown mass thudded onto the jungle floor just past where Jagger had been standing. Jagger's head jerked about, making sure there was nothing else in the trees. Not seeing anything, he cautiously hobbled towards the brown mass he'd just blasted. It was some kind of animal, some kind of primate, lying face down. Jagger kicked it over, getting a better look at the thing.

The creature was a spider monkey. He could see the holes the bullets from his Colts had punched through the animal's small body. Jagger could see too they hadn't been what killed the spider monkey.

There was only a stubby trace of its tail, crusted with dried blood. This monkey was larger than he'd have thought it should be, nearly three feet from head to feet. Something had bitten away most of the lower left side of its body. Sucking in a breath, Jagger spun about again as best he could, turning in a circle, eyes searching the jungle again. The spider monkey hadn't come at him on its own. No, something else out there, certainly much larger and stronger, had hurled its corpse in his direction.

He wasn't alone. Jagger could feel something watching him.

"You want me, you bastards?" Jagger yelled. "Come on and get me!"

The only answer he received was silence. Jagger was tempted to fire off a shot in the direction the dead monkey had come flying from but didn't. Once his ammo was gone there wouldn't be any more. Jagger was going to need every shot he had.

Jagger stood there with the mangled corpse of the spider monkey at his feet. It was the source of the stench that had nearly made him vomit. Maggots crawled through its brown hair, swarming there. He wanted to be away from the dead monkey but held his ground. There remained no further sign of whoever or whatever had thrown the thing at him. Jagger was afraid to move. He was damned sure that it wasn't Izan and the cartel guys who were out there watching him. That meant it had to be either cannibals or some kind of animal. If he showed fear, Jagger knew the odds of being attacked went up. Of course, he couldn't just stand where he was forever.

"Come on!" Jagger yelled again at the jungle. "What the Hell are you waiting for? I'm right here!"

Something moved in the trees in front of him. It tore through them, moving away from him. Whatever the hell it was, Jagger didn't think it was human. Whatever it was, the thing was big and fast, moving with incredible speed. It was there and then it was gone. The noise vanished into the distance as quickly as it had come into being. He hadn't gotten any kind of real look at the thing at all.

Jagger let out a sigh of relief. Whatever the thing out there was, it was gone now.

He waited a second longer, just to be sure, and then got moving. What little daylight he had left was wasting.

****

Izan knelt, examining the prints he had spotted.

Juan towered over him, frowning. Javier, Migel, and Gerald were spread out in a loose formation keeping watch. The jungle was no one's friend and they all knew it.

"You find anything?" Juan's deep voice rumbled.

Nodding, Izan rose to his feet. "Jagger's headed south and he's hurt."

"How the hell can you tell that he's hurt?" Migel asked, wandering over to them.

Glaring at Migel, Izan slid a knife out of the sheath that hung on his belt. "Watch your tongue, amigo," the word sounded like the worst sort of racial slur the way the killer said it, "or I might just be inclined to relieve you of it."

Migel swallowed hard and then raised his hands. "Hey man! I didn't mean. . ."

"Shut the frag up, Migel," Juan barked, moving to shove him further away from Izan and then turned back to Izan.

"Migel has poor manners, my friend," Juan told Izan, "But how do you know that Jagger is hurt?"

"The tracks," Izan pointed at the ground. "You can tell from them that he's limping. Must have banged himself up getting out of the jet."

"Really?" Juan raised an eyebrow.

"Yes," Izan was filled with frustration. "It's a

simple thing for anyone with a bit of experience."

It was questionable which of them was in charge out here. Juan was Marcola's "# 2" in all things but Izan was always the one who dealt with the cartel leader's loose ends unless they could be solved by something such as a simple drive by shooting or the like.

They'd been huffing it through the jungle for a bit over an hour now. Juan had faith that Izan was leading them in the right direction. He'd never trusted the cold blooded killer on a personal level but the big man did trust in Izan's skill.

The day, though drawing to an end, remained hellishly hot. When they'd left the jet, the backup batteries were still providing enough power to keep the air conditioner going. He was sure that wouldn't be the case by the time they returned.

"So?" Juan questioned Izan.

Izan met his gaze. "So what?"

"Should we keep on today or head back for the night?" Juan watched the killer sheath his knife and pull out a pack of cigarettes.

Izan lit up, taking a deep drag, before answering. "We're close. If we push on, there's a small chance we could overtake Jagger before nightfall. Even if we don't though, it's not like the darkness would stack the odds in his favor. He's injured, surely exhausted, and alone."

"It's not Jagger I'm worried about," Juan grunted.

Izan shrugged. "The tribe in this area will be around whether it's night or day, big man. If we're meant to run into them, it'll happen one way or another."

Juan weighed the killer's words for a moment. "What do you think? Truthfully, should we push on now or. . ."

Before he was able to finish the question, Izan cut him off.

"I think we should," Izan told him. "No point in waiting. Besides, waiting only gives Jagger a better chance of perhaps reaching the river. If he does that, we might never catch him."

"The river?" Juan asked.

"The Amazon," Izan laughed. "It's why Jagger is heading south. There is purpose to the direction of his flight. As I said, if he reaches it ahead of us, Jagger can use it to make good on his escape for sure."

"It's settled then," Juan boomed. "We keep going at as fast of a pace as we can manage."

"After you," Izan smiled, motioning the big man on ahead.

Juan didn't argue. He endured Izan's contemptuous attitude.

"What are you slackers waiting for?" Juan barked at the rest of the group. "You heard the man. Let's get moving. Gerald, take point. Javier, I want you bringing up the rear. Everyone stay sharp. Odds are we aren't out here alone."

Gerald took the lead with Juan, Izan, and Migel spread out slightly behind him. Javier hung further back as he'd been ordered to. The group moved at a brisk yet cautious pace. The last rays of the setting sun dimmed, giving way to the darkness of night.

"Hey, boss man," Migel whispered at Juan.

Juan craned his head around. "What?"

"Are there really cannibals around here?" It was clear that Migel was on edge from the tension in his voice.

"Yeah," Juan confirmed. "Yuri said there are reports of some freak tribe around here that really does still eat people."

"That's messed up," Migel shook his head. "I thought all the tribes like that were gone these days."

"Me too," Juan admitted and then shrugged, "I trust Yuri though. The man usually knows what he's doing."

Juan vividly recalled Migel's attack on Yuri just after the crash, scowling, and wished he hadn't mentioned the pilot at all. Migel, for his part, was smart enough not to bring up anything about the crash and Yuri's skills as a pilot again. Giving a grunt, Migel at least pretended to accept what Juan said as the truth then fell quiet again.

Suddenly, Izan stopped ahead of them.

"What's up, man?" Migel asked.

"Shush," Izan ordered.

Gerald had paused too, realizing the others were no longer following him.

"We're being watched," Izan warned.

An arrow came streaking out of the trees. It struck Migel in the center of his throat, piercing it to the point that its barbed head protruded out beneath the base of his skull. The poor bastard hadn't even had time to scream. The AK-47 he was carrying slid from his hands as Migel's body collapsed.

"Get down!" Izan shouted as more arrows flew from the trees. They came at the group from every direction. Juan threw himself to the ground, flattening out there, as arrows zipped through the air over him. Gerald ducked behind the trunk of a tree. An arrow thudded into it right next to his face.

Howling in rage and fear, Gerald spun, diving towards another tree. Javier screamed as an arrow hammered into his right leg and he sunk to one knee.

Izan had drawn the sword strapped to his back with seemingly impossible speed. It slashed through an arrow from the air as it flew at him, then another.

A chorus of angry shrieks echoed around the group as the attack upon them truly began in earnest. Half a dozen tribesmen burst from the trees to their right while five more came at them from the left. Some of the cannibals wore the tattered, filthy remnants of modern clothes which had likely belonged to the last people from the outside world who wandered through their turf. The rest were barely clad wearing only loincloths covering their genitals and necklaces made of clattering bones. They were armed with knives, clubs, and spears.

Izan made no move to draw his pistols. Instead, he met the cannibals in their charge, engaging them with his sword. The katana's blade flashed in the moonlight before drawing blood. It removed the head of the closest cannibal to his position, sending it bouncing along the jungle floor as a geyser of blood erupted from the stub of the neck where it had been attached.

Xavier's UZI roared to life, hosing the cannibals coming in from the right flank with a stream of fully automatic fire. Three of them were hit by his barrage, bodies jerking about as bullets tore at their flesh.

Gerald worked the pump of his 12 gauge, chambering a round. He leveled the weapon at a cannibal wearing ratty, torn pants, with a knife raised up above him, ready to strike. The blast sent the cannibal flying backwards, his abdomen blown open. Purple, red slicked strands of the cannibal's guts poured out of him as he rolled over where he had landed, trying to get up. Gerald worked the pump of his shotgun again as another of the cannibals hopped onto his back. The savage had an arm around Gerald's throat, squeezing tightly, both to hold onto him and cut off his breath at the same time. With a fierce grunt, Gerald swung forward, bending over, to fling the cannibal off. The cannibal thudded onto the ground in front of him as Gerald jerked upright, aiming the barrel of his shotgun downward. Gerald's finger pulled the weapon's trigger. The blast of the shotgun flashed in the darkness as the heavy slug that left its barrel reduced the cannibal's face to a mess of gory pulp.

Juan rose from the jungle floor, opening fire with his own shotgun. He worked its pump, firing shot after shot into the ranks of the cannibals. One shot severed a cannibal's leg at its knee joint in an explosion of blood and flying bits of white bone. Another removed the entire left side of a cannibal's face. And his third shot tore a chunk of meat and muscle away from a cannibal's shoulder, sending him reeling about.

Then a cannibal who had slipped up behind Javier grabbed the youth by his hair from behind, yanking his head backwards to expose his neck. The jagged edge of a stone knife ran across Javier's throat. Blood sprayed from the wound as the cannibal released Javier and charged onward at Juan. The big man whirled about, seeing him coming. Juan sent the cannibal to hell with a shotgun blast that punched a gaping hole in the center of the cannibal's ribcage.

Gerald cried out as an arrow imbedded itself in the meat of his upper back causing him to let go of his shotgun. It fell to the jungle floor at his feet as Gerald panicked, trying to reach around far enough behind his own back to get a hold of the arrow and try to pull it loose.

Juan looked in Izan's direction. The killer was

more than holding his own. The corpses of three cannibals lay scattered about him as he fought a forth. The blade of his sword swung towards a large cannibal who wore a blood stained and ripped white shirt above hole riddled blue jeans that were torn apart completely from ankle to knee on one side. The cannibal blocked Izan's swing with surprising skill, bringing up his knife to parry it.

From somewhere deeper in the jungle sounded a thunderous roar, so loud that it seemed to shake the very trees. Hearing it, the cannibals halted their attack as quickly as it had begun, fleeing away into the trees and shadows.

"What the hell?" Juan muttered to himself, attempting to catch his breath. He had never heard anything like that in his life. It had an almost human edge to it.

Izan's blade was dripping blood as the killer shifted into a defensive posture.

Migel and Javier were dead. That took a moment to sink in for Juan. Everything happened so damned fast it almost didn't seem real.

"Help me!" Gerald whined, giving up his attempt to get the arrow that was stuck in his back out on his own, staggering towards Izan.

The killer didn't give a crap about Gerald's plight.

His focus was entirely upon the jungle around them.

"They're gone," Juan said. "Whatever the hell that was scared them off. I don't think they'll be coming back anytime soon."

****

Jagger had reached the river just before the sunset. The Amazon was an awe-inspiring sight that took his breath from him. It was hell not to just dive into the river and drink its flowing water. Jagger knew just how dirty the water was though. There was a risk of parasites as well if he did, not to mention the larger things that could be lurking within it. Piranha, snakes, caiman. . . all could be in there just waiting on him to enter. He had no means of gathering the water in order to strain and boil it either.

Exhaustion overwhelmed Jagger. He stumbled and sat down on the river bank. What the hell was he supposed to do now? Jagger wondered just what his plan had really been. Without a boat or some sort of raft, he was just as screwed here at the river as he had been in the jungle. His best bet was likely just to take the risks and hurl himself into the water. The river's current would carry him further and faster than he could manage on foot. Jagger wasn't ready to go that far yet. He was surrounded by a freaking rainforest. Then he remembered a video he'd watched long ago online. There were smaller streams that flowed down the banks of the Amazon, running into it. All he needed to do was locate one and then follow it up into the jungle to its source. As thirsty as he was, Jagger couldn't force himself to get moving again so soon. He decided to take a few minutes to rest and let the pain in his leg dull some. As he sat there, Jagger just couldn't bring himself to get up again. He remembered another means of getting water from a river. It wasn't by any means as safe as tracking down a spring but desperate times called for desperate measures.

Jagger, sitting aside his pistol, reached and broke a piece of wood from a fallen branch near where he sat. He plunged it into the mud and started digging. His plan was to use the ground itself as a filter for the river water. Scooping away more mud with his hands after getting the hole started, Jagger leaned back and watched the hole fill up. It took some effort but he managed to get down where he could drink straight from the water in the hole. It tasted like crap but felt wonderfully good going down his throat. Thirst quenched, Jagger sat upright, watching the water of the river flowing by. Night had fallen now and the moonlight was reflecting off its surface, making it even more beautiful to behold.

From somewhere in the distance behind him, Jagger heard gunfire. He threw himself flat, making the pain in his leg rip through him with hellish intensity all over again. Face splashed with mud, he lay there listening to the sounds of what had to be a battle. A wry grin spread his lips. The cartel guys, likely led by Izan or Juan, maybe even both, were indeed after him but they'd apparently run into some trouble along the way. The cannibals of the region was Jagger's best guess as to what. He thanked God for not stumbling into them himself and hoped that they eliminated the cartel guys for him. Jagger knew that was unlikely though. Even if the tribesmen had somehow caught them off guard, the cartel guys were armed with modern weapons and Izan himself was like death incarnate. The tribesmen would pay dearly for attacking them, Jagger was sure, but even if they took out only a single cartel thug, it increased his own odds of getting away or even facing them himself if that time came.

Something splashed in the river. Jagger looked up from where he lay, craning his head to get an even better look at the water beyond his position on the bank. There was something out there. Something in the river. He could see a pair of yellow eyes glowing in the darkness. They were staring at him with such primal fierceness that it sent a chill running along his spine. Jagger picked up his pistol from where he'd laid it down, his knuckles going white from the pressure of the grip he clutched it in.

The animal with the yellow eyes was beneath the surface of the water so Jagger couldn't get a good enough look at it to see what exactly the animal was. He figured it was some kind of caiman despite the chilling intelligence in its gaze Whatever the thing might be, Jagger didn't plan on letting it get anywhere near him. Too tired and too injured to simply run, shooting at the thing wasn't a fantastic plan either. If he'd heard the cartel's shots in the distance, there was no reason they couldn't hear his just as well and doing so would lead them straight to him.

Jagger froze, his eyes bugging in pure shock and disbelief. The thing in the river rose up to stand on two feet. Even up to its waist at least in water, he guessed the creature had to stand over eight feet tall. It stood on two legs like a man but wore no clothes.

The scales of its reptilian body gleamed in the moonlight. The thing's arms and legs were thickly muscled like a weightlifter's. Its chest was wide as were its shoulders. A crocodile-like snout extended outward from its face below those glowing, yellow eyes that had filled Jagger with an almost supernatural sense of dread. The creature even had a tail like a caiman, thrashing about behind it in the water. Jagger fought the urge to scream. The thing shouldn't . . . couldn't . . . exist, could it? It was like something out of a horror film come to life in the real world. Then the creature gave a thunderous roar that echoed among the trees of the jungle.

Jerking up his pistol at the monster, there was truly no other name to describe it with, Jagger resisted the urge to make a pathetic attempt at fleeing, and held his ground. The monster advanced slowly with an eerie calmness. Either it didn't know what the pistol he was pointing at it was or just didn't care.

"Stay back!" Jagger yelled.

The monster snorted in contempt as if it understood what he had said but kept moving towards him. Jagger took aim at the monster's head. He was screwing around with going for a body shot. From the look of its scales, a round from his pistol likely wouldn't have the power to penetrate them. Jagger hesitated, not quite pulling the trigger, as the monster took its next step and then. . . it was too late.

Springing forward with impossible speed, the reptilian monster swatted Jagger's pistol from his grasp. The weapon spun through the air, landing several yards away, lost in the darkness. The blow snapped Jagger's trigger finger, nearly ripping it off his hand in the process. Jagger yelped in pain but had time to do nothing else as the monster's other hand darted out to seize him by the throat. Cold, rough fingers closed around his flesh there, choking him. Jagger's training kicked in. He punched the monster in its side with his left hand, summoning up all the strength he could muster. Its scale tore at the skin of his knuckles. It was like punching a brick wall. The monster didn't even seem to notice he had struck it.

The monster effortlessly lifted Jagger up from the river bank into the air. Jagger kicked at its torso with his feet, trying to force the monster into dropping him. The blows had no more effect than his earlier punch to its side. Jagger forced himself to calm down and think things through. It was either that or die. He didn't have the strength to break the crocodile man's hold on him. Risking it all was his only hope. Jagger knew the crocodile's ears were just behind its eyes. He lunged forward, slapping his hands onto the ear slits right behind the creature's eyes.

Jerking its head back in sudden pain, the crocodile man released Jagger. He thudded onto the river bank at its feet and kicked out with his right foot. The kick smashed into the crocodile man's stomach. It didn't hurt the monster but with the crocodile man already staggering, it was enough to send the creature tumbling over back into the river. It splashed below the surface of the water as Jagger clawed his way up the bank and took off running at a full out sprint into the trees.

****

Sparks flew as Yuri cursed and hopped away from the wires he'd been working with. He slammed a fist into the wall of the jet's pilot compartment. Frag it, Yuri thought, there wasn't crap that could be done to repair the comms. He'd figured it was worth a shot though before the last of the power failed and died. The batteries were already near their end. Another hour or so at best and nothing on the jet would work anymore.

Harrison's corpse still sat in the main pilot seat with the limb of a tree stuck through it. The man's decaying flesh stunk like hell in the heat of the jungle. The only place aboard the jet where the air conditioning continued to run, for now, was Marcola's private quarters. The cartel leader had ordered him to find out what he could about the area the jet had crashed in but that was impossible with the comms out. Marcola didn't have enough knowledge of how things actually worked to know that so he was going to be expecting to be told something more. Yuri wasn't going to have anything new to share but there was a plan forming in his head, one that might endanger Jagger but maybe, just maybe, one that could save him too.

With a start, Yuri whirled about as someone entered the pilot compartment behind him. The screwdriver in his right hand was clutched like a weapon before he saw that the person who had come in was Marcola himself. Yuri's eyes went wide. Lowering the screwdriver as quickly as he could, Yuri said, "I'm sorry, sir. I didn't. . ."

Marcola laughed loudly. "I understand your fears, Yuri. I think we are all shaken up from the day's events are we not?"

"Yes sir," Yuri's head bobbed up and down. "I know I am."

"It is okay," Marcola assured him with a smile that had an edge to it. "But you know why I am here."

"I wasn't able to find out much more," Yuri lied. He hadn't found out crap beyond what he'd already known.

Marcola shook his head and clicked his tongue. "You've found nothing?"

"Not about this area," Yuri said and watched the violence igniting in the cartel leader's eyes. "But I think I have a plan that could get us out of here and back to civilization a hell of a lot faster than what we talked about earlier."

The cartel leader relaxed ever so slightly. "Go on then. Tell me about it."

"There's no point in trying to march all the way back through the jungle, sir," Yuri said. "This jet has numerous emergency rafts aboard it. If we. . ."

Marcola stopped him there by taking a step closer and laying a hand on his shoulder. "Yuri, you're a freaking genius. Yes! Yes, what you're thinking is a much fragging better option. We can use those rafts to travel the river."

"Exactly." Yuri did his best to put on a smile

though his guts had gone cold with fear.

Grinning, Marcola turned to leave the pilot compartment. "I shall let the others know about our change of plans, Yuri. We'll leave out at dawn. Get anything that you think could help us along the way ready."

"Will do," Yuri responded.

When Marcola was gone, he slumped into the co-pilot seat, sighing with relief. That had been dang close. Marcola was the sort of guy who would kill somebody for just looking at him the wrong way. Yuri had survived talking with the cartel lord yet again. He knew that was going to keep happening forever even if he wasn't found out as the undercover agent that he was. .

At least, Marcola had opted to wait for dawn instead of driving everyone out into the jungle at night. The river wasn't that far away. The journey to it should be an easy one since they'd be able to see where they were going. Yuri knew that Marcola would be counting on him to lead the way and get them there. That wasn't a problem though. He'd seen exactly where they were in relation to the river as the jet plummeted out of the sky. The river was southward from their position and that was the direction Jagger had fled in. A fact that would also make Marcola happy if Juan and Izan hadn't already come back with Jagger's head by the time the sun had come up.

Marcola had to be wondering where they were. Juan, Izan, and three of Marcola's thugs had been dispatched to find and eliminate Jagger hours ago. Yuri sure had no explanation for why they hadn't returned. There wasn't a chance in Hell that Jagger had taken all five of them out. Both Juan and Izan were forces to be reckoned with on their own; add three armed thugs to them and Jagger didn't have a prayer if they found him. And Yuri guessed that was what had happened, Jagger had hidden himself away somewhere. The only other explanation was that Jagger had somehow managed to reach the river ahead of them and was already long gone but Yuri thought that unlikely.

Yuri heard a commotion from the zone of the plane outside the pilot compartment. There were shouts and a lot of movement. Then Juan's deep voice called out, "Yuri! Get the hell out here!"

Rushing out, Yuri was taken aback by the chaos he saw. The group sent to eliminate Jagger had returned. . . but not all of them. Izan had taken up position at the hole in the plane they'd entered through as if guarding it while Juan was in the process of lowering an unconscious Gerald onto the floor.

"Yuri!" Juan barked. "You're the only one onboard with medical training. Help him!"

Seeing the backside of Gerald's shirt was soaked in blood and moving to kneel next to him, Yuri asked, "What happened?"

"Arrow," Izan snorted without even glancing in their direction.

"I'm thinking it must have been poisoned or something," Juan commented. "Gerald seemed okay at first but got weaker and weaker as we traveled back here. He passed out just a few minutes ago."

The door on the far side of the zone from the one Yuri had emerged from opened. Marcola stood in the doorway there, watching everything closely as it all unfolded.

Yuri tore away Gerald's shirt so he could see the wound. It was bad, deep and the meat savagely torn. He couldn't see any obvious signs of blackening around it or anything else that might indicate poison though. What he did notice was the wound was from more than just a normal, pointed arrow head. The arrow that had imbedded itself in Gerald had to have been barbed and ripped him up as it was pulled out. That was the only explanation for the type of wound he was looking at.

Gerald moaned loudly as Yuri's fingers pressed into and about the wound as he continued examining it.

"The arrow was barbed," Yuri said. "Whoever pulled it out of him shouldn't have. It did more damage coming out than it did going in."

Neither Izan or Juan responded to that.

"But is he poisoned?" Marcola's voice rang out.

Yuri shrugged and shook his head, "I don't see any clear signs of that. Likely him passing out is just a combination of the hellish heat out there and losing so much blood as he has."

"Can you save him?" Juan asked.

"Save him?" Marcola snapped, "What the hell, Juan? We don't have time to play at crap like that. Besides, he was the one who screwed up, yes?"

The cartel leader left where he stood in the doorway of his private zone of the plane and walked over to tower above Gerald. Drawing the pistol holstered on his hip, Marcola pressed the end of its barrel to Gerald's forehead and squeezed the trigger. The backside of Gerald's skull exploded outward in a spray of blood, brain matter, and bone fragments.

Marcola shoved his pistol back into its holster

and looked around.

"Clean that up!" he snapped at a pair of his thugs.

Juan was staring at the cartel leader with rage burning in his eyes but said nothing.

Yuri kept his mouth shut. Gerald's blood had splattered onto him. He felt sick, bile rising in his throat. Swallowing it down, Yuri saw that Izan was still at the hole in the plane's wall. Jagger surely couldn't have taken out two men, wounded a third, and got Izan so spooked. It made him wonder exactly what was out there that Izan was watching for.

"Juan, Yuri," Marcola called, walking through the doorway into his personal quarters. They followed after him. Maria shut the door behind them.

Marcola took a seat on the edge of his bed, looking at Juan and Yuri who stood in front of him. Shonda still sat in a chair near the bed. The room was hot and sweat beaded on her skin. The AC was out now as the jet's backup systems had finally failed, the batteries giving out.

"Tell me," Marcola said with a scowl on his face, "Why you've returned without Jagger and three of my men missing? I'd expected better than that from you, Juan."

"We're not alone here, sir," Juan told him. "The cannibals Yuri told us might be in the area are here. They ambushed us. Migel was dead before we even knew what was happening. They got Javier too."

"I see, Marcola snorted. "But clearly you drove them off, no? You and Izan are still alive."

"We barely got out of there, Marcola," Juan said. "If we had stayed. . ."

"If you had stayed, maybe Jagger would be in my hands now, Juan," Marcola countered. "Or are you seriously going to suggest to me that you and Izan couldn't handle a bunch of primitive idiots with spears?"

"They were using bows," Juan shook his head. "And knew how to take folks out from a distance. If we hadn't gotten out, even Izan would likely be dead now. I am not exaggerating, Marcola. You know me. I've always been loyal and gotten the job done before, haven't I?"

Marcola clicked his tongue. "Here is what's going to happen, Juan. In the morning, we're going to head for the river. All of us. Yuri came up with a plan to get us home much quicker while you were away and we will all follow it. That said, Jagger can't be left out here alive. That's not a risk we can take. His death must be ensured. You and Izan will go after him again. Take more men if you need but no more than that."

"We've lost too many already," Maria commented.

"Yes," Shonda agreed, "Three to cannibals, one in the crash, two turning out to be federal agent scum. . . that's a fragging bunch of us already and the worst is still ahead if you're telling the truth about how dangerous these cannibals are."

Yuri sure as hell didn't call her on saying the cannibals had gotten three and Juan didn't either. Gerald could have been saved but doing so was deemed not worth the effort, time, and resources.

Marcola clapped his hands together. "Enough!"

Everyone fell silent waiting on the cartel boss to speak again.

"Juan. . ." Marcola said, his voice barely more than a whisper, "Do not fail me again."

"I won't," the big man swore. "Jagger will be dead before we leave this jungle. I'll make sure of that."

Marcola's gaze shifted to Yuri. The pilot and undercover agent forced himself to keep calm.

"Yuri, have you completed the preparations for

us to leave at dawn?" the cartel leader asked.

"Mostly," Yuri answered, "There's not much left to do. Just another once over of the jet to make sure we've got everything we might need as you ordered."

"Good, then you are no longer needed to oversee that," Marcola smiled. "I want you to be one of the men to accompany Juan and Izan as they go after Jagger again."

"Sir?" Yuri yelped, not able to hide his surprise at such an order.

"You are the most knowledgeable person here when it comes to this area and what dwells here, Yuri," Marcola's smile fell from his face, the cartel leader's expression growing harder. "I know you are only a pilot but all of us at times are called to action that must be taken when the circumstances are dire. I want you to go with them and give them whatever help you can. Juan and Izan will keep you safe. Right, Juan?"

The big man glanced over at Yuri, frowning, "Yes sir."

It didn't take a genius to know that Juan was only saying what Marcola wanted to hear. Yuri had just seen what had happened to Gerald out there. There was still some of Gerald's blood on him. Still, there was nothing either of them could do but agree with Marcola in order to keep breathing right now.

"I'm going with them too," Shonda spoke up, catching everyone, even Marcola, off guard.

"What?" Marcola snapped, his head jerking around.

Shonda met Marcola's eyes. "You heard me. And you saw how things went for them out there the first time. They need me as much as they need Yuri to guide."

Marcola almost lost his temper, leaping up from the bed. Once he was on his feet though, the cartel leader calmed and then laughed. "Oh Shonda, you are a brave one, child. Go then if you must."

She nodded, a feral grin parting her lips.

"Out now, all of you," Marcola waved them away. "And be ready to move at dawn!"

Juan opened the door for Yuri and Shonda, allowing the two of them to leave first. Once the three of them were outside, Yuri started to head for the pilot's compartment but Juan stopped him, a large, sweaty hand clutching his shoulder.

"No, Yuri," Juan said shaking his head. "You heard Marcola."

"I did," Yuri protested, squirming out of the big man's grasp. "He said we would be heading out at dawn."

"The others will," Juan corrected him. "Night out there or not, we can't afford to lose any more time where Jagger is concerned. Go find yourself a weapon. I'll gather some men to accompany us."

****

Izan was angrier than Juan had been when the killer found out they were leaving the jet before dawn. He stood peering out into the darkness with Yuri and Shonda flanking him.

"Cannibals for real, huh?" Shonda giggled.

The killer glared at her for a moment. "Yes."

"I knew they were supposed to be around but I really didn't think we would run into them," Shonda commented. "And if we did, I figured you'd just handle them like you and Juan do everything else."

"This jungle is their home," Izan told Shonda. "They know it much better than we do."

"Sure," Yuri agreed, "But she means that you're . . ."

Izan almost grinned at that.

"I'm a killer, Yuri," Izan nodded. "But so are they . . . and they have the numbers."

"There can't be that many of them, can there?" Shonda asked.

Yuri watched Izan's response closely, trying to get a feel of what the professional killer was really thinking.

Izan shrugged. "Again, this is their home. There could be dozens or there could be hundreds. We won't know for sure until it's too late if they decide to come at us in force."

"Damn," Shonda muttered.

"So we could be royally screwed if we stumble into their village," Yuri commented.

Juan marched up to them with two more of the cartel soldiers in tow. Yuri recognized them as Saul and Christo. Saul was a burly man. The kind that you could look at and know to be a fighter. He had the swagger of one too, full of himself and always ready to use his fists. Christo, in sharp contrast, was as tall as Juan but lacked the giant's muscles that made him the hulking force that he was. Instead, Christo was rail thin with pale skin and keen eyes. Christo was carrying a rifle with a scope mounted above its barrel. In Saul's hands was an AK-47. Both of them were quiet and sullen like men who knew they were going to war.

"Izan," Juan greeted the killer.

"Juan," Izan nodded in return. "What we're about to do is far from the smart move."

"Marcola doesn't give a damn, Izan, and you know it," Juan sighed.

"But if we get to slaughter some primitive natives along the way, it just might be fun," Shonda quipped.

"Let's just go find Jagger and get this over with," Juan sighed.

Yuri had armed up too like Juan had told him to do. He'd raided the jet's small armory and picked out an UZI for himself, an extra mag for it crammed into his pocket. That wasn't all Yuri had gotten though. He'd gotten a 9mm Glock as well as a backup weapon.

Izan sighed. The professional killer moved aside and gestured for Juan to lead the way. "After you then."

Juan had to squeeze through the hole in the hull. Saul and Christo were next.

Yuri noticed Izan's eyes on him.

"Marcola is making a mistake by sending you," the killer commented.

"You're preaching to the choir there," Yuri smiled.

"What about me?" Shonda smirked. "No concern for my welfare, Izan?"

"You can handle yourself, Shonda. Yuri though,

he's sending him to his death," Izan said bluntly.

"Uh. . . " Yuri stammered, "I sure as hell hope not."

"Understand now, my job is not to babysit you out there, Yuri," Izan told him.

"Yeah, I got it," Yuri answered and climbed out of the jet. It was a short drop onto the jungle floor. The night air was cooler outside but still humid as hell.

Shonda moved to lean in close to Yuri and whispered, "Don't you worry. I got your back out there."

Yuri barely managed not to yelp as Shonda squeezed his butt before walking away.

Juan and his two thugs were already moving deeper into the jungle. Shonda was ahead of him too. Yuri hurried after them knowing that Izan would be on his heels even if he didn't see or hear the killer. Before he caught up to Juan though, Yuri turned to look back at the jet. It was a miracle the thing hadn't completely been broken apart. Both of its wings had snapped away and the tail section was barely intact. The rest of the jet's hull was bashed up with a few spotted holes here and there but otherwise had somehow held together. Harrison and himself had really done one hell of a job bringing her in. Yuri took pride in that as his gaze drifted upwards. The night sky was full of bright stars. It was beautiful but in such a manner that it made one aware of just how small they were in the grand scheme of things.

"You'd better keep your eyes on the things around you, Yuri," Izan cautioned, stepping out of the shadows to appear directly in front of him.

Yuri didn't say anything back to the killer. He just nodded and got moving. He and Izan caught up to Juan and the others easily. The five of them spread out with Izan remaining in the rear. Yuri could tell Juan wasn't happy about that. It would have made more sense in some ways to have the professional killer, given his instincts, on point. Izan wasn't having it though and Juan wasn't going to fight him over it.

The group moved at a brisk pace with Juan in the lead. The night was far from quiet. The jungle was alive with the cries of night creatures moving about, hunting their prey. Yuri was creeped out by it all. He felt so very vulnerable and exposed. On a night like this, they might never see or hear a threat until it was right on top of them.

Without warning, Izan sprang towards him, the killer's sword leaving its sheath. Yuri screamed as its blade flashed through the darkness, gleaming in the starlight. Something wet and warm splattered onto him. Then at his feet lay the head of a snake. The thing's body was close to ten feet long, blending in near perfectly with the foliage around it. Yuri hadn't seen it at all, even as the snake struck at him.

Yuri looked at Izan who was in the process of wiping the blade of his sword clean.

"Thanks," he muttered.

"I warned you to be careful, Yuri," Izan smirked. "Next time, I might not feel like stepping in to save your life."

Yuri stared at the corpse of the beheaded snake. He shivered despite the heat, thinking about what could have been were it not for Izan. God only knew what other horrors were in the darkness waiting.

"Best not to think about it," Izan told him.

Shaking his head to clear it, Yuri knew the killer wanted him to keep his place at the rear. He left Izan behind with the dead snake, watching the trees around him for anything else that might be lurking in their branches.

The hours passed like days as they trudged through the jungle. The sun was beginning to come up, its first, early rays seeping through the trees. Everyone was relieved to see the light. There were still plenty of threats in the jungle but at least now they all had a better shot at anything coming their way. .

They came to a stop.

"This is where we were attacked yesterday," Juan said.

"Quite a spot," Shonda knelt, examining the jungle floor as if she were a tracker. Yuri bloody well knew she wasn't.

"Migel and Javier's bodies are gone," Izan pointed out.

"Yeah," Juan nodded, "I noticed that."

"The cannibals?" Saul asked.

"You can bet on it," Juan answered.

"Is that one always such an idiot?" Shonda gestured at Saul.

Saul glared at her with pure hate in his eyes but kept his mouth shut. Everyone knew whose side Marcola would take in a fight if it came down between them and Shonda. You didn't mess with Marcola's women if you wanted to continue breathing.

"Frag," Christo shook his head in disgust. "That's just wrong. I mean what kind of people actually eat other people?"

"Ain't nothing right about this place," Juan agreed.

"So where do we go from here?" Yuri asked.

"I thought Marcola sent you along so that you could tell us that," Christo smirked.

"Leave him be," Juan barked.

"We go south," Izan spoke up. "Just like we had been yesterday."

The professional killer walked past them all, taking the lead for the first time since they'd ventured out of the wreckage of the jet during the night. Juan happily let him take point.

Yuri was sweating and from more than just the heat and all the walking. He was on edge and had been ever since the incident with the snake. It was hard to believe that he was marching through a jungle filled with cannibals. That had never been part of the plan. He was supposed to already be in the States seeing Marcola and his crew brought to justice. If Marcola ever began to suspect that Roberto and Jagger hadn't been the only agents planted in his crew, he'd be just as dead as Roberto already was and Jagger was likely to be soon. . . assuming the jungle hadn't done the job for Juan and Ivan.

****

Jagger collapsed onto the jungle floor. His wounded leg hurt so bad that he was on the verge of passing out. It felt like he had been running forever. Jagger kept moving as quickly as he could throughout the night, pushing himself to his limits and beyond them, but couldn't any longer. There was no sign that the monstrous thing from the river was following him and he prayed to God that the creature was far behind him. His flight had been a blind one. Jagger didn't have a bloody clue where he was. . . but he could still hear the river in the distance. He'd managed to keep near it somehow. Jagger wasn't sure if his zig zagging path had doubled him back to it or if he had unconsciously simply run parallel to its course. That was perhaps the most worrisome thing to Jagger at the moment. The monster lived in the river.

His gun was gone. The creature had knocked it away from him, leaving him weaponless. And his leg was more messed up than ever. The wound had miraculously stopped bleeding so that was a good thing. He couldn't walk his way out of the jungle. Jagger knew only death was ahead for him if he tried. The only real option left to him was using the river and letting it carry him in its current but. . .

that meant getting in the river, where the monster surely lived.

Something snapped in the trees to his right. Jagger's head jerked around expecting to see a humanoid crocodile pouncing on him. There was no monster though. Squinting against the sun, Jagger couldn't see anything amidst the trees. That didn't mean there was nothing there. Something had made the noise he'd heard, be it human, animal, or monster.

Jagger's eyes scanned the jungle floor around where he lay, searching for something, anything to use as a weapon. He found a fist-sized rock, partly buried in the damp soil. Clawing it up, Jagger steeled himself for a fight. If something was about to try and take him out, he was going down easily.

A sharp twang that could only be the release of a bow string reached Jagger's ears seconds before he screamed in fresh pain. An arrow came flying out of the trees to bury itself in the meat of his right shoulder. It pierced him deeply there, barbed tip protruding outward behind his back from where it had gone all the way through. He didn't dare drop the rock clutched in his hand. His fingers gripped it tighter in response to the pain and his determination.

A series of primal shouts erupted in the foliage around Jagger. It wasn't the monster that had found him but the cannibals. Jagger almost breathed a sigh of relief at that realization. Against other humans, he stood a chance, or so he hoped.

Jagger watched as a man wearing tattered, filthy, blood stained pants emerged from the trees. He was carrying a wicked looking primitive knife, grinning beneath hungry eyes. He was only the first to reveal himself. From the west came two more like the man but wearing nothing more than loincloths and necklaces made of bone. One of them was carrying a bow, a quiver of barbed arrows strapped to his back. The other wielded a small, stone ax. Those were the only weapons Jagger could see.

They were cannibals. Had to be based on what he knew of this region. Jagger gritted his teeth as the cannibal with the ax circled him. The other two held back, watching. Picking his moment, the cannibal with the ax yelled and sprang forward at him. Jagger managed to twist his body out of the path of the swinging ax blade and smash the rock he clutched into his attacker's knee. Bone crunched from the blow. The cannibal yelped and toppled. He went down on the damp jungle floor next to

Jagger. Seizing the chance while he had it, Jagger raised the rock again, bringing it down onto the side of the cannibal's skull. Where the rock hit, the cannibal's skull folded inward with a sickening, wet, cracking sound. Blood flowed from the cannibal's nose and ears as his body twitched and spasmed, thrashing about in his death throes.

The other two cannibals held their ground. Neither rushed forward despite the fact that he'd just killed their buddy. Jagger figured the one in the beat up tatters of modern clothes was their leader and met his eyes. They stared at each other in silence. Jagger kept his expression hard and violent. Seconds ticked by.

Finally, the lead cannibal reared his head back and shrieked, an almost inhuman cry. Several more of the tribe burst from the trees, all charging Jagger. They carried various weapons ranging from spears to knives. Jagger screamed as the first to reach him thrust a spear into his left thigh. Blood spattered up and out from where its tip entered. Another of the cannibals darted in to slash open the side of his shoulder. Jagger swung, striking back, but missed. Then the hand of a third cannibal roughly grasped his hair, pulling his head back atop his neck. Jagger felt the jagged, stone blade of the knife that killed him as it tore open his throat. Blood flowed in rivers of red down over his chest as more spurted out of his neck with each beat of his heart. The world spun before his eyes and then. . . there was only darkness.

****

Juan had stopped ahead of the rest of the group, bringing them all to a halt. Yuri's eyes bugged as he heard Jagger's voice cry out in the distance. It was filled with such pain . . . Shuddering, Yuri clutched his UZI tighter.

"What the Hell?" Christo barked. "Was that him?"

"Sure as hell sounded like him to me," Saul commented.

"Who else could it be?" Shonda huffed at the two of them, clearly thinking they were idiots.

"Everyone just hold up," Juan ordered though Izan was already gone.

"Too late for that," Shonda smirked. "Izan was outta here in the blink of an eye."

"Screw him," Juan growled. "If he wants to go off half-cocked and get killed out here, that's not on me."

"Uh. . .boss," Saul said.

"What, Saul?" Juan was angry and getting angrier at the position Izan going ahead on his own had left them in.

"Forget it," Saul answered. "Let's just do whatever it is we're going to do."

Yuri, listening to them all talk and argue, kept out of it. He didn't want to take any chance of giving away his real identity by accidently responding to something wrong. Even professionals like himself slipped up sometimes in situations as stressful as what they were facing.

"Okay," Juan worked the pump of his shotgun. "Christo, Shonda, I want to you edge off the right. Yuri, you and Saul take the left. I'm going straight up the middle. You see anything that isn't Izan, blow the bloody hell out of it."

The group surged forward in unison. No one knew what to expect. Yuri kept his finger ready on the trigger of his UZI and his eyes open wide.

Yuri and Saul were the first of the group to enter the clearing. Jagger was lying on the ground in a pool of his own blood. There was a savage primitive squatting over him, slashing open Jagger's stomach with a crude knife. The man gutting Jagger had to be one of the cannibals in the area and he wasn't alone. There were several of his fellow tribesmen in the clearing too. Some of them at least had heard the group coming and were ready. One released an arrow that streaked through the air, spearing into Saul's shoulder. He screamed, losing his grip on his AK-47. The weapon toppled from his hands to land in the tall weeds of the jungle floor. Yuri let loose with his UZI, hosing the closest of the cannibals. A cannibal staggered backwards, struck by nearly a dozen rounds, each sending splashes of blood splattering as they tore into his flesh. Another took only three rounds but they punched gaping holes in the side of his face and neck. A third was struck by a round to his right arm causing him to drop the bow he'd used to attack Saul. Yuri let up on the trigger, swinging his UZI around as he heard a shout from behind him. He turned but not fast enough. The rough side of a wooden club smashed into his jaw. Teeth and blood flew out of his mouth as the impact jerked his head sideways. The world went fuzzy before his eyes. Yuri slumped onto his knees as the cannibal that struck him raised his club again for the killing blow. It never fell though. Izan exploded from the trees, sprinting up to the cannibal, separating the tribesman's head from his shoulders with a single slash.

His vision clearing, Yuri saw the rest of the group entering the clearing as more cannibals emerged from the brush across the clearing from them. A cacophony of gunfire erupted. Juan's shotgun thundered. Shonda's AK-47 chattered, and Christo's rifle boomed in rapid succession. The first wave of the charging cannibals were dead in seconds. The suddenness of their massacre caused the others behind them to stop their charge, turning tail to flee back the way they had come which did little to save them. Yuri couldn't truly see how many got away but he saw another half dozen fall to the group's continued barrage of heavy fire. Then as quickly as it all had begun, it was over.

Juan was looking around to make sure none of the cannibals had cut around to come back at them as he worked the pump of his shotgun, chambering a fresh round. Christo knelt down to him as Yuri shook his head. It was clearer now but his jaw hurt like hell.

"You okay, man?" Christo asked.

Yuri managed a nod as he probed the bloody gums where two of his teeth had been with his tongue. He was surprised that it was Christo who was checking on him. Yuri barely knew the guy and Christo sure didn't come across as the most caring of people.

"They gone?" Yuri heard Shonda ask. Her voice dripped with excitement and bloodlust left over from the short battle.

"Yeah," Juan confirmed. "For now, anyway. I'd wager we scared the crap out of them."

"You got lucky," Izan commented. "Things could have gone much worse."

"Frag," Juan whirled on Izan, the big man towering over the lithe killer. "You're the one who just took off, Izan. What the hell was up with that, just leaving us like that?"

"I had a job to do," Izan answered flatly.

Izan gestured towards Jagger's corpse. "And it's done now."

"Little help here?" Saul pleaded, clutching the shaft of the arrow that was sticking out of his shoulder.

Christo was smirking as he said, "Bet that hurts like a. . ."

"Don't yank it out," Juan warned before Christo could finish what he was saying.

"I wasn't planning on it," Saul assured the big man.

"We do need to get it out though," Yuri heard himself say.

Yuri looked at Chirsto, "Help me up."

Christo offered a hand that Yuri used to pull himself to his feet.

"Wait," Izan barked, drawing everyone's attention to him. "Something's not right."

"What? Are they coming back?" Juan snapped, still looking about the edges of the clearing and not seeing any indication that the cannibals were there.

"No," Izan shook his head, "This is something else. Something. . ."

The only warning that was given was the blur of movement as the creature burst from the trees. It was on Saul before anyone, even Izan, could react. The creature wore no clothes though it moved on two legs like a man. It was shaped like a man too for the most part, two arms, two legs, a head but the resemblance ended there. Standing at around eight and half feet tall by Yuri's best estimate, the thing was all scales and thick muscle. Its eyes burnt a demonic red, hot and full of violence. The front of its face was like that of a crocodile's, a long snout-like mouth extending outward which opened, showing rows of razored teeth, in the moment before it snapped shut on the lower half of Saul's face. Bone crunched, shattering and giving way to the amount of pressure being exerted on it as the thing's teeth pierced and ripped through Saul's flesh. Saul hadn't even had time to scream. The creature wrenched its head away in a sharp jerk, tearing what was left of Saul's entire jaw away with it in an explosion of blood. Saul staggered backwards, eyes wide, blood pouring from where the lower portion of his face had been. There was another crunching sound as the creature chewed upon the contents of its mouth.

Izan sprang into motion. The lithe killer was leaping towards the monster before Saul's collapsing body had landed on the jungle floor. The blade of Izan's katana flashed, arcing through the air towards the creature. The blade thudded into the thick scales of its neck. Unable to penetrate them, it skidded downward against the scales before bouncing harmlessly away. The killing strike Izan intended in reality did nothing more than anger the creature. It lashed out, backhanding the killer. Izan grunted in pain as he was lifted from his feet by the blow and sent flying into the trunk of a nearby tree.

Juan's shotgun boomed but the creature was already moving again. The shotgun blast splintered the bark of a tree behind where it had been a second before. Yuri swung his UZI up in the creature's direction but it was already too close to Christo for him to have a clear shot at it. A scaled hand closed around the barrel of Christo's rifle, shoving it skyward, as the weapon barked. The creature had messed up the only shot he was likely to get it. Christo was screaming, attempting to tear his rifle free from the grip that held it. A blast of fire from Shonda's AK-47 struck the creature in its side. Only a few of the rounds drew blood, not all of them penetrating the armor of the creature's scales. The damage they did however was still enough to save Christo's life. Thrusting out a hand, the monster knocked Christo from his feet, sending him toppling over flat onto his back. Unholy eyes burning with anger, its head turned in Shonda's direction. She fired a second series of bursts at the monster but this time the thing had seen them coming, flinging its huge form out of their path with seemingly impossible speed.

Yuri cut loose with his UZI spraying a stream of fully automatic rounds at the monster as it retreated back among the trees. The bark of several trees cracked and splintered as the bullets hammered into them. The monster was already deeper in the jungle, sprinting away from Yuri and the others.

"What the hell was that thing?" Shonda shouted.

"Some kind of freaking mutant maybe," Juan shrugged.

"No," Izan grunted, rising to his feet. "It was the Crocodile Man."

The big man glared at the sword-wielding killer.

"What's the Crocodile Man?" Yuri asked, fresh sweat, born of fear, glistening on his skin.

Before Izan could respond, Christo cut in. "Whatever the frag that thing is, it killed Saul."

Christo was kneeling next to Saul's corpse, his expression one of boiling rage.

Rubbing at the growing bruise that was forming on his face, Izan still managed a scowl. "That thing was the Crocodile Man," he said again. "Apparently it's much more than just a local myth."

"I'd say so," Shondra huffed. "That thing was as real as it gets."

"You keep calling it the Crocodile Man like we should know what that means," Yuri stammered. "You're going to have to fill the rest of us in, Izan."

It was Juan who answered, his voice gruff, "The Crocodile Man is a local monster, sort of like Bigfoot in the United States. Folks have reported seeing it for decades or more but no one has ever been able to prove it exists."

"The legend of the Crocodile Man is much older

than just a few decades," Izan corrected Juan. "There are those who believe its legend and the legend of the Alligator Man are just variations on the same creature."

"Wait," Yuri blinked, "there's an Alligator Man too?"

"That's not what he said," Shondra shook her head. "He said that there are two legends but one monster."

"Yes," Izan nodded. "The Alligator Man is a story of a pervert who used to watch women bathe in the river. In order to do so, he obtained a magical potion that could alter him from being a human being into an alligator so he need not worry about being caught during his "pleasures". Only one day, things didn't work and the potion messed him up, turning him fully into a monster and not just an alligator or man but a hybrid of both."

"Ugh," Shondra cringed. "So that thing isn't just a monster, it's a perverted freak too?"

"That is only one story," Izan answered. "The other, which I believe holds more truth, is that there was once a mighty warrior among the cannibals who live in this region. It is said that he approached the dark gods of this jungle and traded his humanity for the power to live forever, being assured never to die in battle so that he could go on killing forever."

"If that story is real, it would mean that. . ." Yuri shuddered.

"The creature we just fought is immortal," Izan said. "Yes, I know."

"Nothing is immortal," Juan spat. "That's a load of pure crap. Hell, Shondra tore that fragger up with her AK and sent it running."

"It was bleeding," Christo pointed out. "Juan's right. If the thing bleeds, we can kill it."

"I didn't say it couldn't be hurt, Juan," Izan glared angrily at the big man, "I said it couldn't be killed. We are in great danger out here. You can count on the Crocodile Man coming at us again. Now that we've hurt it, our fates are sealed unless we can escape this jungle before. . ."

"All that crap you're talking, Izan. . ." Juan grunted, "…it's just crap and all of us know it. That thing might be a monster but it's not supernatural or immortal."

"Then what is it?" Izan pressed. "You call it a monster but if it was not born of magic, where did it come from?"

"Hell, toxic waste, radiation, some kind of covered up government project that got loose, you name it, man. There are a ton of others thing it could be than this mystical creature you're claiming it is," Juan protested. "Who knows? Maybe it's a fragging alien!"

Izan frowned. "It is none of those things and you can feel it just like I do."

Juan laughed. "What are you, some kind of psychic ninja now or something?"

Sighing, Izan responded, "Regardless, we are all in grave danger. We must get moving before the Crocodile Man returns."

"Look, guys," Shondra interjected, "we know the thing is out there now. That means we'll be ready for it next time."

Yuri looked up at the sky. "The sun will be coming up soon."

"Jagger is dead," Izan stated coldly, walking over to where the man's corpse lay on the jungle floor. He brought the blade of his sword down in an arc onto Jagger's neck. Jagger's head separated from his body. Izan clutched it by its hair, lifting the head up.

"Good thinking," Juan's deep voice rumbled. "Marcola will want proof."

"Indeed," Izan agreed.

"Guessing we got less than an hour to dawn,"

Juan commented. "We'll never make it back to the others by then."

"Marcola planned to get everyone else out and on the move as soon as the sun came up. Do you think he'll wait for us?" Yuri asked.

Shondra laughed. "Marcola does what's best for Marcola. That's a fact. With the news you guys brought back about the cannibals in the area last night, despite what he said, I'll wager Marcola is still holed up in the plane, waiting on us to return. No matter how much he wants to be on the march for home, Marcola won't make a move unless he thinks it's safe to do it. With you two," Shondra gestured at Izan and Juan, "both out here, odds are he isn't about to trust his life to the low level thugs we left with him no matter how well armed they are."

"Let's hope you're right," Juan sighed. "Okay, everyone. The clock's ticking and daylight's coming. Izan, if you'd be so kind as to take point."

Izan stared at Juan for a moment but in the end didn't argue with the giant. He tossed Christo Jagger's head, which was still dripping blood, then got his bearings before heading off into the jungle in the direction of the plane. Everyone else followed after him with Juan bringing up the rear.

****

The thick bulkhead doors to Marcola's quarters were closed and slicked with a red wetness that dripped from them onto the expensive carpet covering the floor of the room. It had taken the last of the plane's power to shut them. That meant the lights and air conditioning of his quarters were things of the past. Marcola was trapped inside the room with the temperature rising. His skin was drenched with sweat that ran from his dark hair into his eyes, stinging them. Wiping at his face with the backside of his right hand, Marcola was breathing heavily. His years of being the head of his cartel had taken their toll on him. Once, he'd been as lean and tough as Izan . . .well, almost anyway. Now, Marcola was older and used to being pampered. He was still very much a fighter and would be until death claimed him, but Marcola was well aware his edge had been lost long ago. That fact was all that saved him when the *thing* had come. It tore into the plane without warning. The first of his men that Juan had left to protect him died without even being able to scream. The creature burst through the hole in the side of the plane, grabbing the man, smashing his head into a shower of exploding pulp against the metal wall. That was when the gunfire started. The other two of his thugs took their shots at it. The closer of the two was armed with a shotgun. It boomed like thunder inside the wreckage of the plane. The blast caught the monster in its scale-covered chest, sending it staggering backwards as the other thug jerked up the 9mm pistol he was armed with. The pistol cracked over and over in rapid succession, each round it fired striking the monster and bouncing harmlessly away. The monster recovered, lunging forward. The thug working the pump of his shotgun to chamber a fresh round died as the monster's fist caved in his face, bone crunching beneath the force of its blow.

Maria was screaming next to him as she and Marcola watched it all happening. He'd known their only hope was getting the doors of his quarters sealed and hoping that they held against the monster's rage. And the thing was truly a monster. Marcola had never seen anything like it in his life before. It stood over eight feet tall, all reptilian scales and violence, yellow eyes burning with primal rage. The last man defending him popped the spent magazine of his pistol, slamming another one home as the monster came tearing through the plane at him. Marcola knew the man wasn't going to be able to stop the monster or even buy him enough time to get the doors sealed. Maria's squeals and screams were only making things worse and messing with his ability to think clearly. He'd had enough.

As the monster slapped the pistol away from the thug that had been shooting it, Marcola grabbed hold of Maria, slamming her down into the metal floor outside of his quarters, making sure she struck it hard enough to stun her. Marcola spun about, going to work on the control panel on the wall near the doors. The last thug died, the monster effortlessly lifting him up into the air. His body parted along its midsection, spraying blood and guts as the monster ripped him apart.

Maria, shaking her head to clear it, looked up and saw the doors of his quarters closing. Marcola had finally managed to get the override code entered into the panel. The lights were flickering and dying but the heavy doors were sliding closed. Maria shrieked, trying to lunge through them as the monster came sprinting towards her. Marcola saw its clawed, far too humanlike, hands clutch her shoulders even as the doors closed on her extended right arm which was reaching for him as she cried out his name, begging for help. As the doors severed Maria's arm, blood splattered everywhere, as the part of it that was inside his quarters thudded onto the floor at Marcola's feet. He could feel her warm blood on his cheeks and face. Marcola had staggered back away from the doors, able to hear Maria screaming still beyond them. Her screams didn't last long. . . then it was all over, just as quickly as it had begun. Darkness had enveloped him as the lights went fully out. The AC and everything else too. Marcola felt the edge of his bed against the backs of his legs and dropped to the floor, leaning against it. There was a pistol holstered on his hip but Marcola didn't bother to draw it. He had seen how useless 9mm rounds were in stopping the thing outside. If it got inside with him, he was dead. He sat there in shock as the monster rammed into the doors several times. They shook but didn't give. With each of the monster's attempts, Marcola felt like vomiting. Then, the monster's attack on the doors simply stopped.

Marcola didn't have a clue how long he'd been sitting in the dark but it seemed like an eternity. His head was in his hands, eyes closed, as he waited for help to come. The group Juan and Izan had taken out were supposed to be returning by dawn which wasn't long away. Of course, trapped in his quarters as he was, Marcola wouldn't be able to see the sunrise or know that it had happened. The room had no windows. He resented his fate being left in the hands of underlings, even ones as trusted as Juan and skilled as Izan. There was nothing he could do though. Though he hadn't heard the monster outside the doors in some time, that didn't mean the thing wasn't lurking there, merely waiting on him to emerge. If he could emerge, that was. The doors keeping the monster out also kept him in. If and when Juan's group did come looking for him, they would not only have to face the monster but devise a means of forcing the doors open as well. His quarters, Marcola realized, had perhaps become his tomb. It wasn't in his nature to cry and even less so to beg. He was raised Catholic. In his heart, Marcola knew that God was real. It didn't mean he was about to start praying. Marcola despised himself deep down on an unconscious level and projected those feelings onto God, blaming the creator for all that was wrong in the world. There was no way in hell that Marcola would bow his head or kneel to some being that had in his mind wronged him all his life.

Straightening up where he leaned against the side

of his bed, Marcola took out a zippo lighter from his pocket and flicked it lit. The light illuminated the room around him. There wasn't much to see. At least nothing that would help him in his current situation. Pulling himself up to his feet, Marcola used the light to find a bottle of wine and opened it. Lifting it to his lips, he chugged the wine as if it were beer. A wave of anger washed over him. Marcola threw the bottle into the far wall of the room. It shattered there, shards of glass breaking and bursting apart. Destroying the bottle did nothing to calm Marcola. If anything, it just enraged him more. Jerking his pistol from the holster on his hip, he turned and stared at the sealed doors of his quarters.

"Damn you, you fragging monster!" Marcola shouted. "Damn you to hell!"

****

Yuri, Izan, Juan, Shondra, and Christo stepped out of the thickness of the jungle into the area where the plane had crashed. The sun was up now. Its rays were still weak but continuously growing brighter and stronger. The heat was already intense and the humidity seemed to never end. All of them were sweating profusely and were worn out from the fast-paced hike racing against the sunrise.

"Thank God," Shondra huffed. "Looks like they haven't set out yet."

"That's because they're dead," Izan frowned.

"What?" Juan bellowed.

"What the frag you talking about?" Christo blurted out.

"Can't you smell it?" Izan told them. "The blood and decay in the air."

"Shut the frag up, Izan," Juan grunted, marching on towards the plane. Yuri and the others rushed after him with only Izan holding back.

As they closed on the plane, Yuri smelt it too. They all did. Juan gagged at the smell, stopping in his tracks.

"Damn!" Juan covered his mouth and nose with one hand, keeping a firm, ready grip on the shotgun he was carrying now with the other. His huge form stood motionless as he stared into the darkness of the plane's interior where the smell was coming from.

"Believe me now?" Izan asked, walking quickly by the big man and the rest of the group to position himself between them and the plane.

"Don't mean nothing," Juan shrugged. "Could just be an animal or something that got in there after they left and died."

Izan sighed and shook his head.

"You don't think. . ." Christo stammered. "You don't think that thing got them and is in there, do you?"

"No, if the creature was still here, it would have attacked us already," Izan said calmly.

"How do you know it wasn't the cannibals?" Shondra asked.

"Look at the ground to your right, Shondra," Izan instructed her.

She did. Shondra's eyes bugged, noticing the massive, deep track in the muddy jungle floor for the first time. She flinched and then leaped away from the track as if it were a live snake that was coiled up to strike at her.

"Bloody hell!" Shondra shrieked.

"Hey!" Christo shouted at her. "Didn't you hear Izan? That thing ain't here anymore! We're safe."

"He didn't say that," Juan countered. "You only said it wasn't here, right Izan?"

The professional killer nodded. "That's correct. As I have said, none of us will be safe until we are out of this jungle."

"Someone needs to go in there and check things out," Shondra gestured at the plane. "We have to know if Marcola's dead or not, don't we? If he got out and finds out we didn't make an effort to save him, we're all just as six feet under as if that monster got its claws in us."

"You volunteering?" Christo smirked at Shondra then turned suddenly serious, "Cause I sure as hell ain't going in there."

"I'll go," Yuri spoke up.

Everyone's eyes turned to him. Juan and Izan shared matching expressions of surprise.

"You?" Izan challenged him.

"Yep, me," Yuri frowned. "It's time I contributed something, right?"

A feral grin formed on Izan's lips as Juan nodded and said, "Sure, Yuri. You want the job, you got it. Get in there and see if anyone's left alive. Give us a shout if you run into trouble."

Yuri walked the rest of the way to the plane where the crash had torn a hole in its side. As he reached out to clutch the metal, already hot to the touch from the sun's rays, Yuri sighed. Offering to go in wasn't the most ideal thing to keep his mind off the worries that were haunting him but it also allowed him to earn more trust from the others. That was something he needed desperately until they could all get out of this hellscape and back to the real world. Yuri wondered if Izan had already pieced together exactly who and what he was. If so, the killer was keeping it to himself for the time being but sooner or later, Izan would either clue the rest in or just take his head off with that funky ninja sword of his. With Jagger and Roberto dead, there was no one left to help him out here. He was alone, surrounded by enemies, most of which would end his life in a second if they knew his secret, and as if that wasn't enough, there was an honest to goodness monster hunting them too.

Being an undercover Federal agent was always a risky job, full of danger, but Yuri had never imagined he'd be in this kind of trouble. Between the three of them, he, Jagger, and Roberto thought they had things covered and bringing Marcola to justice was going to be a cake walk. Well, at least possible without getting themselves killed. Things sure as hell hadn't played out that way. Yuri didn't know exactly how Roberto had been found out but one slip had set everything else in motion . . .and now here he was spending every moment praying for just another hour alive and not to be found out.

Yuri pulled himself up into the plane's interior. As soon as he did, Yuri saw the first corpse. He could see from the dim rays of the sun spilling through the hole behind that the man's head was gone. It appeared to have been smashed to pulp against the metal of the plane's wall. There were three more dead bodies in sight between him and the doors that led into Marcola's quarters. The plane's power was out for sure. Not even the emergency lights were working. Yuri was carrying a flashlight attached to his belt. His hand reached for it and turned the light on. The others had died violently as well. Yuri felt the burning sensation of bile and vomit rising up in his throat. Through sheer willpower, he fought it away, keeping his focus on his job and his surroundings. One of the bodies was Maria. Most of her clothes had been ripped away and her legs were spread widely, bones broken where they met her pelvis. Deep gashes, clearly made by clawed hands, covered her body. The bulk of her right arm had been severed off above its elbow. But the worst was how her forehead sunk inward. Something had struck it with enough force to shatter and cave in the bone of her skull there. The pressure that blow must have created inside Maria's head had popped her eyeballs mostly out of their sockets. They protruded out of them, horrid and grotesque. Yuri knew he would never be able to forget the sight of them for as long as he lived. There was nothing to cover her or the other corpses with. Their smell was just as terrible as how they looked. The heat and humidity inside the plane was just as bad if not worse than it was outside in the jungle. Flies swarmed around and above the corpses, buzzing everywhere. Poor Maria. Yuri didn't really know her but no human being should ever be made to suffer like she surely had. He didn't want to think about all Maria must have endured before the Crocodile Man finally ended her life. Yuri shuddered and did his best to get his mind centered back on his task of finding out if Marcola was still alive.

Stepping over Maria's mangled and broken body, Yuri approached the doors to Marcola's quarters. They were splattered with blood that likely mostly belonged to Maria. It must have taken the last of the plane's power to get them closed. It would certainly explain why the emergency lights were out. Looking at the bodies behind him and the doors, Yuri was beginning to piece together what must have happened. The Crocodile Man must have slipped inside, took out the guards before they even had a chance to react to it, and then went for Marcola. Knowing the drug lord, Marcola had likely sacrificed Maria to give him time to get the doors sealed. It would have taken some time to override the normal systems and do it. Either that or Maria had just been really unlucky and the monster had gotten its hands on her before Marcola could manage to seal the doors but that didn't seem likely. The question now was whether Marcola was still alive in his quarters? Was the Crocodile Man trapped in there with his corpse? That was possible if the monster had gone inside while the doors were closing. Yuri had seen how strong and powerful the monster was. Even so, he didn't think even it could tear through the doors. They were built tough as hell, to withstand explosives and turn Marcola's quarters into a sort of panic room. But whoever or whatever was inside the room would surely be trapped there because the doors on the room's other side would have sealed too. There would be no way out until one of the sets of doors were opened which wasn't going to happen with the plane's systems out of power. Well, that wasn't entirely true. Roberto had shown him a few tricks on how to get them open but they weren't things he could manage by himself. If he and Juan worked together though. . .

As Yuri stood there, he heard a dull thumping sound. It startled him, nearly making him leap out of his skin. The noise rang out again and he quickly realized it was coming from behind the sealed doors. There was really someone or something alive beyond them. That meant Marcola had to be alive and trapped. If whatever was in there had been the Crocodile Man, Yuri imagined the pounding on the doors would have been much louder and more violent. Taking a breath and calming down, he headed back out of the plane to let the others know what he had found.

"Well?" Juan asked as soon as Yuri dropped to the jungle floor. "I take it they're not in there. . .at least not alive."

"Marcola and the others never made it out here," Yuri answered.

Izan snorted, "The smell told us that much already."

Juan ignored Izan's comment.

"Weird footprint in the mud or not," Christo spoke up, "we don't know for sure that thing out there is what killed them. It could just as easily have been those cannibal freaks."

"It wasn't," Yuri assured him. "It was the Crocodile Man. Tore in there, hit them so fast and hard, they didn't stand a chance."

"What about Marcola?" Shondra blurted out

though there was no real concern for him in her voice.

"Not sure," Yuri answered honestly. "There's someone or something sealed up in his quarters behind the emergency blast doors. I heard a noise from in there."

"And you didn't check that out?" Christo gave him a sharp look.

"He couldn't," Izan said before Yuri could respond.

"What the hell do you mean he couldn't?" Christo challenged the lithe killer.

"The power's out, you idiot. The back ups must have finally given out," Juan barked, looking as if he was resisting an urge to bop Christo in the back of the head. "Those doors won't open without it."

"So what do we do now?" Yuri asked, not daring to take the lead on anything.

"We go in there and find out if Marcola's still breathing," Juan huffed. "Whether he's dead or he made it out, we have to make sure of what happened either way."

"Juan is correct," Izan nodded. "Yuri, do you know of a way we can open the doors to his quarters without power?"

"There's a manual override crank but it's not easy

to get to and it'll take Juan to turn the thing," Yuri told the killer. "If even he can."

Juan grunted as if insulted. "You get me to it and I'll get it done."

"Fair enough," Izan smirked. "Let's be about it then. Time is not our friend."

The group headed into the plane with Izan in the lead. While Yuri and Juan went to work on doing what was needed to get the doors to Marcola's quarters open, Shondra knelt by Maria saying a prayer over her body. Christo remained by the hole they had entered through, his eyes watching the jungle for any sign of the monster or the cannibals. Izan disappeared into the pilot compartment without saying another word to any of them.

Izan returned by the time Yuri and Juan were set up to open the doors. The killer was carrying a flare gun. Yuri wondered what Izan was planning to do with it but didn't ask. He turned his gaze back to Juan at the override crank.

"It's ready to go when you are," Yuri told the big man.

The banging against the other side of the doors had started again and was growing louder as Juan threw all his strength into opening them. The doors slowly opened.

"It's about fragging time!" Marcola raged at them. "It's hot as hell in here!"

The drug lord came stumbling out as soon as there was room for him to slip through. "I thought I was going to die from the heat before anyone ever showed up!"

"Sorry, sir," Juan answered, frowning.

Shondra threw herself at Marcola, taking him into a tight embrace. Though she acted her part well, Yuri was very well versed in deception himself and knew she was faking it.

"What happened here, Marcola?" Izan questioned the drug lord.

"Some sort of monster. . . " Marcola answered as if forcing the words out. It was unlike the drug lord to be shaken by anything but something had scared the crap out of him. That much was clear. "It got inside the plane and killed everyone else. If I hadn't gotten those doors closed. . ."

Marcola caught himself, eyes narrowing, and suddenly snapped at Juan, "Just where in the hell were you people anyway? I needed you here."

"We were doing what you sent us to do," Izan replied, voice calm and flat, despite Marcola's outburst. "Jagger is dead. I left his head outside but it's there if you need to see proof."

Marcola straightened up to his full height, putting on a show of pride and dignity. "Good. I hope he died very painfully and slowly."

"The cannibal tribe that resides in this region actually got to him before we did," Juan admitted. "They got a bunch of us too as you can see. We're all that's left."

The drug lord's expression twisted into a fierce snarl. "Well I suppose I should be grateful to them for taking out Jagger for us but I hope you sent those bastards to hell too."

"Some of them," Juan said.

"Not enough," Shondra pulled away from Marcola, releasing her hold on him. "There are too many still out there. . . just like that monster, they could come for us at any time."

Marcola flicked his head sideways, popping his neck. "Juan, Christo, get the cargo ready for transport."

Juan stared at the drug lord in disbelief. "Sir?"

"Did I stutter or something?" Marcola huffed. "You heard me."

"But sir," Juan protested. "With the cannibals and the monster out there. . ."

"Have you lost your mind, Juan?" Marcola bellowed, "I don't give a damn about what we're up against. We are not leaving a fortune in narcotics in this jungle to rot!"

Yuri was keeping quiet, not about to get involved in the argument. Juan was right. Trying to haul Marcola's drugs with them would only slow them down and get every single one of them killed but there wasn't crap he could do about it. He was the low man on the totem pole, being just a pilot. Not to mention his desperate effort to keep from being found out. Yuri swallowed hard as he saw the drug lord looking directly at him.

"Izan," Marcola smirked.

"Yes," Izan answered, stepping closer to the drug lord.

"While I was trapped in that hell hole, I had some time to think," Marcola cackled as if the trauma had made him crazier than he had been. "And you know what I realized?"

Izan cocked an eyebrow and merely waited for the drug lord to continue.

"Aren't you curious, Izan?" Marcola grinned. "No?"

Still remaining quiet, Izan watched Marcola carefully.

"You see, I figured out that those bastard Feds weren't alone," Marcola said. "There wasn't just two of them. There were three."

Shondra, who had been listening to the conversation, keeping her mouth shut like Yuri, spoke up.

"Marcola. . ." she started.

The drug lord laughed loudly. "That's right, my dear, I figured it all out. You're the third fragging spy they sent to get me."

"What?" Shondra cried out, stunned by the accusation, taking a step back. "You're insane!"

"Izan," Marcola smiled. "If you would be so kind as to dispatch her."

"My pleasure," Izan responded though his face was utterly emotionless. Drawing his sword with lighteing speed, Izan swung his blade around.

Juan had reluctantly started into Marcola's quarters towards the cargo that was in the section of the plane beyond them but he'd heard what was being said and turned around. He saw what was happening but there was no hope of stopping it. Nonetheless, he shouted, "Izan! No!"

The lithe killer's blade removed Marcola's head from his tanned shoulders. The drug lord died in a splash of hot, wet blood that splattered onto Izan and Shonda. Marcola's head went bouncing away from his body.

In the seconds that followed, Juan and Christo swung their weapons up, trained on Izan. Shondra moved to stand beside the killer, her gun aimed back at them. The killer had just saved her life, after all. It made sense for her to take his side.

"Wait!" Yuri screamed, diving between them all, arms up and extended. "Everybody just calm the hell down!"

"He killed Marcola!" Juan raged. "You know what that means, Yuri. He just signed our fragging death warrants!"

"It had to be done," Izan said, voice as calm and flat as ever. "You know it did."

"Frag you, you bastard," Christo spat. Christo likely would have pulled the trigger of his weapon right then and there if Juan hadn't reached out and placed a hand on top of his AK, pressing its barrel downward.

"Hold up," Juan ordered him.

Christo's head jerked around at his boss, eyes wide. "What the hell, man?"

"I hate to say it but what's done is done," Juan told the thug. "And if we don't all work together, none of us are getting home anyway."

Izan allowed a thin smile to form on his lips.

"Listen to Juan," Yuri urged Christo. "We need

you, man. We need all of us to even have a chance of getting out this jungle alive. We can deal with the rest later."

"Fine," Christo snarled. "I want to know though," His eyes turned to Shondra. "Are you really a Fed?"

"Hell no!" Shondra raged.

Yuri noticed Izan steal a glance at him and knew that the killer was no fool. Yet, Izan said nothing, returning his attention to watching Christo. If the thug made a foolish choice in the next moment, his life would end just as Marcola's had.

Sweating from more than just the heat, Yuri reached up with a trembling hand to wipe at his brow. He didn't have a clue why the lithe killer didn't just go ahead and take him out too. If Izan really knew he was a Fed, what the hell was he waiting for?

"What's done is done," Juan said again, firmly and loudly. "Now we all need to get our heads back on straight and start coming up with a real plan to keep ourselves alive."

"Our only hope is to make it to the river." Shondra was clutching her AK-47 so tightly that her knuckles were white.

"Agreed," Izan nodded.

"But first," Juan gestured towards the rear of the plane, "we need to load up on anything and everything we can that might help us out there."

"Then let's be about it," Izan urged. "Every minute spent here is that much less daylight we have."

****

Fifteen minutes later, the group was on the move, trekking southward through the jungle. All of them except Izan were now carrying a backpack stuffed with water, extra ammo, and more. The only thing the lithe killer had taken from the plane that he saw were the flares he had gotten before the crap with Marcola hit the fan. Yuri still had no clue what Izan had planned for them but the killer never did anything without a good reason.

Juan and Izan were both on point together. This time it was Christo that was bringing up the rear. Yuri and Shondra walked along, side by side, in the middle of the group. The heat and humidity only increased as the day wore on. There were no rest breaks though. Couldn't chance them. Every second had to be spent pressing on as fast as possible towards the river.

The group ate their lunch on the move. Shondra

gnawed on a power bar while Juan and Christo devoured a plastic bag of beef jerky. Izan didn't eat at all. Yuri was left wondering how the lithe killer was able to keep moving. It seemed like he wasn't even human at times. Yuri, himself, had found some salt and vinegar chips on the plane. He tore open their bag and shoved a handful into his mouth.

"How the hell can you eat that crap?" Shondra made a disgusted face, waving a hand as if to ward off the chips' odor.

"I guess they're kind of an acquired taste like beer," Yuri chuckled. "You want one?"

He raised the open bag towards her.

"Hell no, I don't want one," Shondra slapped it away, nearly knocking the bag from his grasp.

"Hey!" Yuri chided her.

"You're an idiot Russian," Shondra shook her head. "You realize that those things are going to dry you up, right? In this sun and heat, moving like we are, you'll burn through the water you're carrying before the sun sets."

"I'm hoping we will have made it to the river by then," Yuri inclined his head in a slight nod at her. "If we haven't, running out of water will be the last thing I'll be worried about."

Shondra suddenly laughed, surprising him. "Ha!

Good point. Still, those things smell like crap so keep your fragging distance with them. I don't want to get sick from their stink."

Yuri found himself laughing with her. They shared a smile as he said, "Okay. I can do that."

Crunching on another handful of chips, Yuri finished up the small bag and tossed it away into the growth of the jungle. He shrugged off his pack, carrying it in front of him while digging out a plastic bottle of water. Having gotten it out, he slung his pack onto his back once more. Still smiling, Yuri unscrewed the bottle's lid and used part of its contents to wash the odor of the chips from his hands. Shondra was watching him in nearly dumbfounded amazement.

"You really are an idiot Russian," she grinned.

"You said the smell was making you sick," Yuri shook his head. "Just doing my best to be a good person."

"Yep. Idiot," Shondra said. "Being a good person will get you killed in our line of work."

"That's not how I see it," Yuri told her. "I keep you from getting sick and you just might return the favor by keeping me alive later on."

"Ah," Shondra purred, "An honest gentleman. I thought your breed died out a long time ago."

"I'm not either of those things," Yuri argued.

"Sure," Shondra grunted. "Whatever you say, Russian."

"You know my name is Yuri," he frowned.

"So?" Shondra shrugged and smiled.

Yuri sighed and changed the subject.

"How did you end up working for Marcola?" he asked.

"How does anyone end up doing what we do?" Shondra's smile became a frown. "Either you're desperate or crazy."

"And which one were you?" Yuri met her eyes, wishing he hadn't asked when he did. There was a profound sadness in them.

"None of your business, Russian," Shondra huffed. "Now how about shutting the hell up already? We've wasted enough energy flapping our jaws as it is."

Yuri nodded. They marched on through the jungle in silence.

****

The sun was sinking in the sky as the exhausted group reached the village. They had stumbled onto it on their route to the river. Izan and Juan had brought them to a stop at its outer edge. The group kept hidden in the trees and vines as they looked it over. The place was like something out of a nightmare. There were people strung up, upside down, with their skin mostly or fully sliced off, blood draining into crude, handmade urns beneath where they hung. The way the bodies were hung was very practical for draining them but even so had almost a ritualistic look to it. But the bodies of the cannibals' victims were far from the only ones in the village. All across the village, scattered about, were the corpses of dozens of the primitive tribe. Men and women, even their elders and children appeared to have been slaughtered by something that must have moved through the village like a hurricane with such speed and power that none of them, even their hardened warriors, had stood a chance in hell against it. One warrior, guts ripped open, exposed to the sun and air, with a broken spear next to his body, lay not more than ten feet from the foliage where Yuri was crouched down.

"What the hell happened here?" Christo whispered to no one in particular.

"What do you think?" Juan grumbled. "Look at this mess, man. It had to be that Croc thing. Nothing else could have done this."

"God in heaven help us," Yuri heard Shondra

mutter beneath her breath too quietly for the others to hear.

"Look at that," Izan pointed towards the center of the village. A crudely carved, wooden effigy of the Crocodile Man stood there, caked with the dried blood of who knew how many of the cannibals' victims.

"These poor bastards must have worshipped that thing like a god," Juan commented.

"Yeah, if they did, then why the hell did it kill them?" Christo challenged the big man.

"From the looks of things," Juan continued to look around at all the corpses, "that thing was in some kind of fragging berserker rage or something."

"That actually makes sense," Shondra interjected. "If it was pissed that it couldn't get at Marcola in the plane and wasn't ready to take us on, the monster must have come here to vent its anger."

"Damn. . ." Christo said, drawing the word out slowly.

It was all nearly too much for Yuri as Izan led them out of the jungle into the village. The lithe killer had his sword drawn and ready though it seemed that the monster who had done all this was long gone. The group spread out, alert and ready for trouble, checking out the horror the monster had left in its grisly wake.

Yuri paused over the body of a young boy. The child's head had been knocked askew atop his neck, barely still attached to his body, hanging on by nothing more than a few strands of sinew. The sight pushed him over the edge of what he could endure. Yuri dropped to his knees, vomiting up the contents of his stomach.

"I bet you're regretting those nasty chips now," Shondra remarked from behind him.

When his body stopped heaving, Yuri wiped his lips with the backside of his right sleeve and accepted the hand that Shondra offered. She helped him get him on his feet again.

"Maybe," Yuri managed a weak smile. "But I'll never admit it."

"Jeez. . ." Christo was shaking his head. "That thing killed the entire fragging village."

"Over here!" Juan yelled. The group gathered around him. He stood pointing at the jungle floor in the dying light of the sinking sun.

"Hmmm...." Izan mused. "Someone got away."

Juan shook his head. "I don't think so, at least not like you mean."

Izan shot him a questioning look.

"The tracks. . . they look more like whoever left

them just walked out of here. They'd be deeper if whoever made them were running," Juan said. "These guys just marched out of here."

"I don't get it," Christo knelt down to touch one of the tracks. "That doesn't make any sense. I'd be running like hell if that thing was after me."

"The monster wasn't after them," Izan looked at Juan who appeared to get what the lithe killer was suggesting.

"No," Juan nodded. "It wasn't chasing them, they were going after it."

"Come again," Shondra was as puzzled as Yuri was.

"They must have been a hunting party," Izan explained. "They weren't here when the Crocodile Man swept through and massacred these bastards. Must have come back and found everyone dead just like we did only they didn't stick around to mourn or dig graves."

"They headed right back out to find and kill the monster," Shondra concluded.

"Exactly," Izan said.

"Frag. That sucks," Christo scowled. "That means we still have them to worry about too."

"It does indeed," Izan confirmed.

"Can you tell how many of them there are from

the tracks?" Juan asked the lithe killer.

"No more than you," Izan shrugged. "My best guess is perhaps a dozen, maybe less."

"That was my thought too," Juan agreed.

"Looks like they're headed south just like we are," Izan sighed.

"You think we'd catch a break sooner or later," Christo frowned. "This fragging jungle is cursed, man!"

"The sun is almost down," Shondra commented. "I know we need to be moving but. . ."

"We're close to the river," Juan's deep voice rumbled. "We have to be."

"Hell, man, we have to keep moving or it's game over like it was for these freaks," Christo snapped.

Yuri finally joined in, saying, "It'll be even more dangerous than it is now to keep moving. Maybe we should just hole up and wait for the sun to come up again."

"Where?" Juan stepped over to him. "Just where in the hell do you think we should hole up, kid? We're in the middle of a fragging jungle. There's nowhere out here except this place. Look around, those huts and campfires did a good job keeping these bastards safe, didn't they?"

The intensity in Juan's eyes eased as he seemed

to catch himself. He frowned.

"Sorry, Yuri," Juan sounded angry at himself. "It's not your fault we're trapped in this Hellhole."

"Maybe it is," Christo cut in. "It was his crappy piloting that got us here. Hell, what if Marcola was right and there is a third Fed here?"

"You'd best stop right there," Juan cautioned. "None of that crap matters anymore, Christo. We're in this together or we're dead. It's as simple as that. Try to get that through your head."

Christo grunted and looked at the big man. He wasn't dumb enough to take on Juan.

"That junk was old a long time ago, Christo," Shondra showed him her teeth in a feral snarl. "Bring it up again, I'll put a fragging bullet in your brain myself and leave you in this jungle to rot."

"We have to keep moving," Izan said, bringing everyone's attention back to him. "There is no other choice."

****

The sun finished setting quickly. Yuri stumbled through the jungle beneath the light of the stars. With each step pain rippled up and down the length of his legs. Everyone else looked as to be as exhausted and hurting as he was. Even Izan was showing signs of being human. The lithe killer led them on, however. Thus far, they'd been lucky enough not to encounter the cannibal hunting party that had escaped the massacre at their village. There were no signs of the Crocodile Man either.

"Hold up," Christo called to Izan.

The lithe killer spun to face the thug. "What is it?"

"I can't go on, man," Christo rasped. "We gotta stop for a bit."

"I hate to say it but I can't keep going either," Shondra admitted.

Izan rolled his eyes, sighing, knowing there was no point in arguing.

"Five minutes," the lithe killer told them all. "Catch your breath if you can."

Yuri slumped over against a tree, sliding down its trunk to the jungle floor. Shondra dropped into the grass next to him. Christo flat out toppled over where he was standing. Juan and Izan both remained on their feet, exchanging a troubled glance between them.

"I know," Izan nodded before Juan could say anything.

"What are we going to do about it?" Juan asked.

"Nothing for now," Izan stated coldly.

"You really think that's wise?" Juan worked the pump of his shotgun, chambering a round.

"Trust me," Izan said, his voice becoming little more than a whisper.

Yuri was watching them as the lithe killer leaned closer to the big man and kept talking. The shocked expression on Juan's face piqued Yuri's curiosity. He needed to know what was going on.

"Hey," Yuri lurched up from where he sat, walking slowly over to them. "What's going on?"

"We're not alone," Izan cut his eyes towards the trees on the eastern side of the small clearing they were in.

"Don't," Juan stopped him before Yuri could whip his head around to look.

"It's the cannibal hunting party," Izan told him.

"And we're just standing here pretending like we don't notice?" It was taking all of Yuri's willpower not to whirl around and open fire on where he figured the cannibals were hidden in the shadows.

Izan made an effort to calm him, "Easy."

"I felt the same," Juan gave a slight nod. "But I don't think those guys are a threat to us. . .yet."

"I believe they are attempting to make use of our presence here," Izan explained.

"Huh?" Yuri was confused. "You don't

mean. . ."

"I do," Izan smirked. "I'd do the same in their place."

"Yep," Juan raised a huge hand to his lips, stifling a chuckle. "The bastards are using us as bait."

Yuri blinked. "Frag me. For real?"

"It makes sense," Juan looked up at the stars above them in the night sky. "We're the strangers here and they can see how beat up and run down we are. That thing is a hundred times more likely to come after us than them."

"For more than just our apparent weakness too," Izan said. "We are the ones who hurt it. I assure you, that thing wants blood for blood."

"And what? You're hoping they'll help us when the creature shows itself?" Yuri quipped.

"Of course not," Izan snickered. "But there's an old saying about keeping your enemies close. Knowing where these guys are is a lot safer than wandering into an ambush they've set up for us down the line."

"If you say so," Yuri shrugged. "But we need to let the others in on this."

"You honestly think Christo can handle it?" Juan gave him a sharp look. "He finds out and our little ruse is over. You can trust me on that."

"Well, Shondra then," Yuri protested. "You know she can handle it and deserves to know."

"Fair enough," Izan motioned for Yuri to head back over to her. "Just be careful how you tell her. If they see that we're onto them. . ."

"I got it," Yuri promised. He wandered over and slumped back against the tree next to where Shondra was sprawled out on the jungle floor. She sat up as he approached her. Her eyes bugged as Yuri leaned over, embracing her like a lover. Shondra's fists clenched but Yuri whispered in her ear.

"Shhhh...." he said, "We're being watched."

Shondra was a student of subterfuge enough to instantly get what he was doing. Leaning into him, her arms snaked out to embrace Yuri like he was her.

Quickly, he let her in on what Izan and Juan had shared with him.

"That's crazy," Shondra breathed into his ear. "They could attack at any moment."

"Izan thinks it's worth the risk until we can come up with a good plan for dealing with them," Yuri explained.

From how Shondra gripped him more tightly, it

was clear to Yuri that she disagreed.

"It's a foolish risk," Shondra whispered. "What we need to do is out maneuver them and use this to our advantage."

"Shondra. . ." Yuri started but she pulled back, placing a finger gently over his lips.

Walking towards the small clearing's edge at a brisk pace, Shondra didn't look back.

"Hey!" Juan shouted after her. "Where are you going?"

"To the little girl's room," she snapped in response but didn't stop.

Yuri leaped to his feet as Izan approached him.

"What is she doing, Yuri?" the lithe killer asked though Yuri suspected Izan already knew the answer to his own question.

"I have no idea," Yuri answered honestly. "But you'd best be ready because I think the crap is about to hit the fan."

"Damn it," Juan muttered.

****

Shondra left the clearing where the others were resting. She knew the cannibal hunting party was somewhere among the trees. There was no fear in her though, only determination and purpose. All her life, Shondra had allowed herself to end up in positions where she was in service to someone else in one way or another. Done with all that, she was ready to stand her ground, stand or fall, and take matters into her own hands. Her AK-47 hung from her back by its strap. Pretending to be searching for a spot to pee, Shondra's eyes scanned around searching for any sign of the cannibals. She spotted one of them watching her, a few feet away. Using his position as a starting point, Shondra acted as if she were undoing her pants and looked for others of his kind, figuring they wouldn't be too far apart. The effort paid off. There was another close by, not far behind her. She squatted above the grass hoping the cannibals would be dumb enough to take her bait and make a move. They did. A lone female in an awkward position.

The cannibal behind Shondra crept towards her. If she hadn't known he was there, Shondra would never have heard him coming. Stealing a glance in the direction of the other cannibal watching her, Shondra saw that he was creeping closer too. Leaping to her feet, Shondra drew and threw one of the twin knives sheathed on her belt at the cannibal coming at her from the trees in front of her position. Even as it spun through the night, blade gleaming in the moonlight, she whirled around, throwing the other at the cannibal behind her. The first knife thudded home into the throat of the cannibal, silencing him as blood splashed outward from where its blade entered his flesh. The cannibal behind her howled in pain as the second knife sunk into and through the soft skin of his right armpit, severing his axillary artery. The cannibal had raised his spear to strike, leaving it exposed enough to be Shondra's target. He toppled over into the damp jungle grass, losing his grip on his spear, grabbing at the hilt of the knife to pull it out. Before he could manage it, Shondra was on him in a fury. She kicked him in the face, shattering the bone of his nose with a sickening crunching sound. The cannibal slumped back, fully onto the ground and didn't move again. Reaching down, Shondra yanked her knife free of his body. She shoved it into its sheath and slung her AK-47 off her back into her hands. Opening up on full auto, Shondra sprayed the jungle all around her. She wasn't sure there were other cannibals close by but if there were, they needed to die too. Bullets tore at the bark of trees, splintering wood, and ripped at the foliage. A sharp, pained scream made Shondra flash a feral grin. She had hit another of the bastards. Ejecting the rifle's spent magazine, Shondra slammed a fresh one into it and sprinted towards the clearing where she had left the rest of the group. Already, a cacophony of gunfire had erupted from that direction.

All hell broke loose around Yuri as Shondra's killing spree pushed the cannibals lurking around the clearing into action. They came rushing out of the darkness. Juan blew a gaping hole in a cannibal's guts as his shotgun thundered. Izan sprang into motion, dancing into their ranks. Three of them fell as his blades opened up one's throat, separated another's head from the shoulders beneath it, and then plunged together into a third's chest. Christo jerked up the AK-47 in his hands but too late. A cannibal emerged from the trees right next to him, slamming a crude, stone hatchet down onto the rifle. Reeling back, Christo swung the rifle around to parry a second swing from the snarling cannibal. Yuri wasn't faring much better. His UZI nearly cut the first of the tribesmen rushing him in half but then unexpectedly clicked empty. He was forced into a desperate retreat as two more cannibals charged him, their eyes full of almost primal rage and thirst for vengeance as if he'd been the one who wiped out their village.

Yuri let his UZI fall from his hands. There was no time to reload it. One of the cannibals brandished a knife, the other a spear. Yuri knew this fight was about to get very up close and personal. The cannibal with the spear closed on him first, thrusting its blade at him. Yuri sidestepped the attack and broke the spear with a downward chop of his left hand that hurt like hell. His right hand, clenched into a fist, smashed into the cannibal's jaw. The cannibal staggered away from him as the other joined the battle. The blade of his knife swiped through the air at Yuri. It cut into the flesh of his left arm. The wound wasn't deep but it did draw blood. Dropping low, Yuri swept the cannibal's legs from under him. The cannibal thudded onto the ground. There was no chance to finish him though as his compatriot rejoined the fight, leaping onto Yuri. The two of them went tumbling, a mass of flailing limbs. They came to a stop with the cannibal atop him as Yuri fought to get free. Yuri was losing and he knew it. The cannibal struck him with the butt of the knife he now wielded, having drawn it from a sheath on his leg. The blow caused Yuri to see stars and set his ears to ringing. The cannibal raised the knife above his head in a two handed grip, preparing to bring it down into Yuri's chest but something came flying out of the darkness of the jungle. It streaked through the air, spinning end over end, before finding its target. The blade entered the side of the cannibal's neck. Hot blood splashed over Yuri as the cannibal collapsed, falling off of him. Yuri sprang up, grabbing hold of the knife in the cannibal's neck, twisting it there to ensure that he wouldn't be rejoining the battle. The other cannibal had recovered and was on his feet again but didn't stay there long. A burst of AK-47 fire peppered his chest with ragged, bloody holes.

"Shondra!" Yuri shouted as she came into view, emerging from the jungle.

"You can thank me later, Yuri," she snapped at him. "This fight ain't over yet."

And it was true. Though Izan had ended the lives of the cannibals engaging him, Juan and Christo were still in trouble. They were surrounded by the last of the tribesmen, fighting desperately to stay alive. Juan's shotgun boomed again, reducing a cannibal's head to an exploding mess of red pulp and white bone fragments.

Christo grunted as a cannibal got the better of him and thrust the tip of a spear into his stomach. Clutching the spear with both hands, Christo did his damnedest not to let it slide deeper into his body but the cannibal surprised him, letting the spear go. Instead of pressing his attack with the spear, the cannibal produced a knife and leaped at Christo, slicing at him. Christo attempted to dodge but with a spear in his guts it was impossible. The cannibal's blade slashed open the side of his face. Christo howled in fresh pain before the cannibal finished him. The blade flashed again, this time leaving a jagged mess of red meat and spraying blood in its wake, opening up his throat. Christo's corpse fell to the jungle floor at the cannibal's feet.

Izan was closer to Juan than Shondra and Yuri. The lithe killer rushed the cannibals the big man was embattled with. Juan had turned his shotgun into a sort of makeshift club, swinging wildly at the cannibals around him, he was trying to drive them back and keep them at bay. Izan was almost on them when another cannibal burst from the trees, tackling him. The lithe killer's sword went flying out of his grasp. Ever a machine of death though, Izan quickly gained the upper hand as he and the cannibal wrestled on the damp floor of the jungle. Izan jabbed a pair of fingers into the cannibal's windpipe, cutting off his air forever.

With Izan stopped from coming to aid, Juan

fought on, the butt of his shotgun caving in a cannibal's skull with a horrid crunching sound. The move left him vulnerable on his right flank. A cannibal in position to strike at him there thrust out with a spear. It pierced the big man's side. Juan grunted, gritting his teeth against the pain, as he dropped his shotgun and whirled about. He broke the spear in two, yanking it out of his side. Lunging forward at the cannibal who had stabbed him, Juan caught the tribesman with one hand, yanking him closer. Juan plunged the half of spear that had been inside of him deep into the center of the cannibal's chest. The tribesman died as the wood sank into his heart.

An inhuman roar rang out from the darkness. Several lower limbs of the trees near Juan were shattered as the Crocodile Man came raging out of the jungle, tearing through them as if they weren't even there. The monster's eyes glowed with primal fury, burning in the night. Its razor teeth gleamed as the Crocodile Man reared back its head and unleashed another roar. The last cannibal fighting Juan found himself directly in the creature's path. The Crocodile Man grabbed hold of the cannibal and with seemingly supernatural strength ripped him in half from his neck to his groin. The cannibal's body separated in an explosion of blood, gore, and innards.

Izan scrambled to retrieve his sword as the few cannibals thar were left turned tail and ran, disappearing into the jungle. Their god had shown itself and they wanted nothing more to do with it. Juan dug in his pocket, fingers desperately searching for another round to shove in his shotgun as the Crocodile Man advanced on him.

Shondra's AK-47 barked and chattered, spitting a barrage of fully automatic fire at the Crocodile Man. Most of the bullets folded up against or bounced harmlessly away from the monster's armor-like scales. A few drew blood but even so didn't penetrate enough to do real damage. They did however get the Crocodile Man's attention. It spun around, the fury of its burning gaze locking onto Shondra.

"That's right, you fragger!" she yelled at the creature. "Come get some!"

The Crocodile Man started to lunge towards her but Juan jumped onto its back. One of his thick arms coiled about the monster's neck in a choke hold while his other reached to draw a knife from his belt. The big man had flung his shotgun away in his move to grapple the Crocodile Man. The huge monster twisted and shook about trying to dislodge Juan from its back, to no avail. Juan held onto it with all the strength he could muster, knowing that he was almost certainly going to be dead from the effort. His hope was that it would buy the others time to regroup and get their act together.

Trying a new tactic to free itself of the big man, the monster hurled itself backwards into the trunk of the closest tree. Juan screamed as his body was crushed between the Crocodile Man's scaly, thickly muscled bulk and the rough bark there. His ribs gave from the pressure of the impact, collapsing inward into his lungs. Blood spurted out of his mouth like vomit. His grip on the Crocodile Man went limb and fell away. The monster whirled to catch Juan's corpse as he slipped toward the ground and hurled it at Izan. The lithe killer had snatched up his sword and was running, full out, at the monster. Izan leaped sideways, avoiding what was left of Juan.

Yuri managed to find his UZI and was reloading it as Shondra opened fire at the monster again. This time, very few of the rounds she fired struck the Crocodile Man. It ducked behind the tree that was smeared with Juan's blood. As her rifle clicked empty, with a mighty heave, the monster wrenched the tree it had taken cover behind up and out of the ground. Yuri would have never believed such a thing was possible but it was happening right in front of his eyes. The Crocodile Man swung the tree like a baseball. Izan threw himself flat, avoiding being struck directly by it. Even so, its limbs raked across his back. Yuri was far enough away to dodge the tip of the tree but Shondra wasn't as lucky. The tree smashed into her with force like that of a runaway eighteen wheeler. It lifted her up from the ground as her body was impaled upon its branches. Grunting from the strain, the Crocodile Man heaved the tree back around and tossed it away.

"Yuri!" Izan shouted, getting to his feet, "Run!"

Too in shock from watching Shondra die to truly understand what Izan was yelling at him, Yuri finally got his UZI reloaded.

The Crocodile Man snarled as it approached Izan. The lithe killer held his ground, allowing it to draw closer, sinking into a combat stance with his sword held ready. Yuri watched the killer and the monster as they began to circle each other, waiting for one of them to make the first move. He didn't intend the give the fragging monster a chance to strike at Izan but the lithe killer was in his line of fire. There wasn't a hell of a lot Yuri could do until that changed.

It was the monster that struck first. Hurling itself forward, the Crocodile Man sprang at Izan. The lithe killer's blade made contact with the monster's scaly armor three times at different points in rapid succession, first its shoulder, then around to its opposite side, and finally the back around and up to the side of its neck. None of the hits drew blood as metal sparked against scale. Izan's lightning fast attempts to stop the monster had failed. The Crocodile Man plowed into Izan. Knocked to the jungle floor, Izan raised the tip of his sword at the monster as it dropped on top of him. Yuri knew well the tactic Izan was attempting, hoping to impale the Crocodile Man. It didn't work however. The scales covering its body were too tough and the blade snapped underneath the weight of its body instead of piercing it. Izan winced as the weight collapsed onto him and he felt his right thigh dislocate. Still, the killer fought on. He lashed out again and again, jabbing at nerve clusters and its throat in the hopes of hitting somewhere that might at least slow the Crocodile Man.

Izan's flurry of strikes ended as the lithe killer

switched tactics again. His right hand produced a flare, looted from Marcola's plane. Izan lit it by striking the flare against the monster's rough scales. It blazed to life, fire burning and sparks flying. The Crocodile Man tried to heave itself up and away from Izan but he held on, keeping its body close. Izan shoved the flare into the Crocodile Man's side. The monster shrieked as it burned where the fire touched its body. For a moment, Yuri almost allowed himself to believe that Izan could win and kill the fragging creature but that hope vanished quickly. The Crocodile Man wrenched the flare from Izan's hand, breaking several of the killer's fingers in the process, and hurled it away into the night. Izan brought a knee up into the Crocodile Man's groin again, causing the monster to cry out in pain. The monster recovered with the same speed that Izan had shown in his attacks and grabbed Izan by his wrists, slamming his arms to the ground and holding them there.

All of the lithe killer's desperate efforts were in vain. The Crocodile Man's mouth went wide and then snapped shut upon the sides of Izan's head. Teeth punched through the bone of his skull as Izan's body twitched and spasmed. Then the powerful muscles of the Crocodile Man's jaws closed, popping the lithe killer's head like an overripe melon. Drenched in Izan's blood and brain matter, the monster rose to its feet.

Yuri stood, heart pounding within his chest, barely able to breathe, facing the monster alone. His courage left him as the monster reared back its head and issued an inhuman roar that seemed to shake the very jungle around them. Yuri turned and ran like Hell. His legs pumped beneath him as he launched himself into the jungle. Pressing his body to its limits and beyond, Yuri ran faster than he ever had in his life. He ducked low lying limbs and jumped over the roots of larger trees that protruded upwards through the jungle floor. Branches scraped at him, raking the exposed flesh of his cheeks, but Yuri ignored them, keeping up his speed. He sucked in a deep breath, realizing that there was no sound of the monster crashing through the jungle after him. Yuri didn't dare stop but prayed his ears were telling him the truth.

Minutes later, the trees in front of him ran out, giving way to a steep bank. The Amazon River lay beneath it, water churning and white. Yuri tried to skid to a halt but saw that he wasn't going to be able to in time. His hand grabbed for something, anything to help break his momentum and bring him to a stop. They found the limb of a tree at the edge of the bank and latched onto it. Yuri swung outward, above the water, and then back around, his feet finding purchase. He carefully made sure that his footing was stable before letting go of the tree limbs. Yuri looked at the palms of his hands. They were bloody and torn to shreds. His gaze shifted to the river. He'd made it. Against all odds, somehow he had. But what now? He had no boat and there was no one else around.

From somewhere behind him came a sharp, hissing noise. Yuri saw that the Crocodile Man had followed him, after all. The monster came slouching through the jungle at an unhurried pace as if sure there was no way its prey, him, could escape it. He realized with a start that his UZI was gone. Yuri couldn't remember where or how he'd lost it.

The Crocodile Man was sneering, showing him its razor-sharp teeth as it approached. Yuri hurriedly looked about for a weapon. There was nothing to be found. When the monster reached him it was going to be a fists to claws fight and he knew which of them was going to win it.

Yuri stood frozen where he was watching the monster's every step towards his position. Then suddenly, the Crocodile Man surged forward with a roar, the muscles beneath the scales of its thick arms and legs rippling. Waiting until the last possible moment, Yuri grabbed the tree limbs next to him and swung out of the monster's path. The act tore his palms up even more, gouging and tearing, making the wounds deeper but it also saved his life. The Crocodile Man went by him out into the open air above the water and fell into the river below. There was a loud splash as its heavy form broke the water's surface. There wasn't a chance in hell that the fall had killed the monster but it had vanished into the river. Yuri dropped back onto the edge of the bank, hands bleeding and stinging. Drops of red splattered onto the mud at his feet. He stood there waiting for the monster to burst up out of the water but it didn't. Seconds ticked by like hours and minutes like years as he continued to watch. Still, there was no sign of the Crocodile Man. The monster was simply gone. Whether the current of the rapids had swept it along and out of the area or it had chosen simply to let him live, Yuri would never know because he never saw it again.

Eyelids fluttering open, Yuri woke up to see the sun rising in the sky. He must have passed out while still watching for the Crocodile Man to emerge from the river. The long night was over and a new day had begun. Hauling himself up to his feet, Yuri knew it was time to find a way home. He set out, following the river, heading south. Sooner or later, Yuri hoped he'd either reach civilization or bump into someone who could take him to it.

End

Author Bio

Eric S Brown is the author of numerous book series including the Bigfoot War series, the Psi-Mechs Inc. series, the Kaiju Apocalypse series (with Jason Cordova), the Crypto-Squad series (with Jason Brannon), the Homeworld series (With Tony Faville and Jason Cordova), the Jack Bunny Bam series, and the A Pack of Wolves series. Some of his stand alone books include War of the Worlds plus Blood Guts and Zombies (from Simon and Schuster), Casper Alamo (with Jason Brannon), Sasquatch Island, Day of the Sasquatch, Bigfoot, Crashed, World War of the Dead, Last Stand in a Dead Land, Sasquatch Lake, Kaiju Armageddon, Megalodon, Megalodon Apocalypse, Kraken, Alien Battalion, The Last Fleet, and From the Snow They Came to name only a few. His short fiction has been published hundreds of times in the small press in beyond including markets like the Onward Drake, Black Tide Rising, and 1632 anthologies from Baen Books, the Grantville Gazette, the SNAFU Military horror anthology series, and Walmart World magazine. He has done the novelizations for such films as Boggy Creek: The Legend is True (Studio 3 Entertainment) and The

Bloody Rage of Bigfoot (Great Lake films). The first book of his Bigfoot War series was adapted into a feature film by Origin Releasing in 2014. Werewolf Massacre at Hell's Gate was the second of his books to be adapted into film in 2015.The Walmart corporation adapted his story the Babble Creek Monster into a short cartoon for their private TV network as a Halloween special. Major Japanese publisher, Takeshobo, bought the reprint rights to his Kaiju Apocalypse series (with Jason Cordova) and the mass market, Japanese language version was released in late 2017. Ring of Fire Press has released a collected edition of his Monster Society stories (set in the New York Times Best-selling world of Eric Flint's 1632). In addition to his fiction, Eric also writes a comic book news column entitled "Comics in a Flash" as well a pop culture column for a newspaper called the Biltmore Beacon and another for an online magazine called Altered Reality. Eric lives in North Carolina with his wife and two children where he continues to write tales of the hungry dead, blazing guns, and the things that lurk in the woods.

Check out other great
Cryptid Novels!

P.K. Hawkins

THE CRYPTID FILES

Fresh out of the academy with top marks, Agent Bradley Tennyson is expecting to have the pick of cases and investigations throughout the country. So he's shocked when instead he is assigned as the new partner to "The Crag," an agent well past his prime. He thinks the assignment is a punishment. It's anything but.Agent George Crag has been doing this job for far longer than most, and he knows what skeletons his bosses have in the closet and where the bodies are buried. He has pretty much free reign to pick his cases, and he knows exactly which one he wants to use to break in his new young partner: the disappearance and murder of a couple of college kids in a remote mountain town.Tennyson doesn't realize it, but Crag is about to introduce him to a world he never believed existed: The Cryptid Files, a world of strange monsters roaming in the night. Because these murders have been going on for a long time, and evidence is mounting that the murderer may just in fact be the legendary Bigfoot.

Gerry Griffiths

DOWN FROM BEAST MOUNTAIN

A beast with a grudge has come down from the mountain to terrorize the townsfolk of Porterville. The once sleepy town is suddenly wide awake. Sheriff Abel McGuire and game warden Grant Tanner frantically investigate one brutal slaying after another as they follow the blood trail they hope will eventually lead to the monstrous killer. But they better hurry and stop the carnage before the census taker has to come out and change the population sign on the edge of town to ZERO.

Check out other great
Cryptid Novels!

J.H. Moncrieff

RETURN TO DYATLOV PASS

In 1959, nine Russian students set off on a skiing expedition in the Ural Mountains. Their mutilated bodies were discovered weeks later. Their bizarre and unexplained deaths are one of the most enduring true mysteries of our time. Nearly sixty years later, podcast host Nat McPherson ventures into the same mountains with her team, determined to finally solve the mystery of the Dyatlov Pass incident. Her plans are thwarted on the first night, when two trackers from her group are brutally slaughtered. The team's guide, a superstitious man from a neighboring village, blames the killings on yetis, but no one believes him. As members of Nat's team die one by one, she must figure out if there's a murderer in their midst—or something even worse—before history repeats itself and her group becomes another casualty of the infamous Dead Mountain.

Gerry Griffiths

CRYPTID ZOO

As a child, rare and unusual animals, especially cryptid creatures, always fascinated Carter Wilde. Now that he's an eccentric billionaire and runs the largest conglomerate of high-tech companies all over the world, he can finally achieve his wildest dream of building the most incredible theme park ever conceived on the planet... CRYPTID ZOO. Even though there have been apparent problems with the project, Wilde still decides to send some of his marketing employees and their families on a forced vacation to assess the theme park in preparation for Opening Day. Nick Wells and his family are some of those chosen and are about to embark on what will become the most terror-filled weekend of their lives—praying they survive. STEP RIGHT UP AND GET YOUR FREE PASS... TO CRYPTID ZOO

Check out other great
Cryptid Novels!

Hunter Shea
LOCH NESS REVENGE

Deep in the murky waters of Loch Ness, the creature known as Nessie has returned. Twins Natalie and Austin McQueen watched in horror as their parents were devoured by the world's most infamous lake monster. Two decades later, it's their turn to hunt the legend. But what lurks in the Loch is not what they expected. Nessie is devouring everything in and around the Loch, and it's not alone. Hell has come to the Scottish Highlands. In a fierce battle between man and monster, the world may never be the same. Praise for THEY RISE : "Outrageous, balls to the wall...made me yearn for 3D glasses and a tub of popcorn, extra butter!" – The Eyes of Madness "A fast-paced, gore-heavy splatter fest of sharksploitation." The Werd "A rocket paced horror story. I enjoyed the hell out of this book." Shotgun Logic Reviews

C.G. Mosley
BAKER COUNTY BIGFOOT CHRONICLE

Marie Bledsoe only wants her missing brother Kurt back. She'll stop at nothing to make it happen and, with the help of Kurt's friend Tony, along with Sheriff Ray Cochran, Marie embarks on a terrifying journey deep into the belly of the mysterious Walker Laboratory to find him. However, what she and her companions find lurking in the laboratory basement is beyond comprehension. There are cryptids from the forest being held captive there and something...else. Enjoy this suspenseful tale from the mind of C.G. Mosley, author of Wood Ape. Welcome back to Baker County, a place where monsters do lurk in the night!